Dear Reader,

Come on. Admit it. At one point in time you have caught a snippet of *The Bachelor*, or *The Bachelorette*, or *Average Joe* or *Who Wants to Marry a Millionaire*? Or maybe you're a dedicated viewer. Well, this story is for everyone who has watched those shows and been amazed that reality can be so...dramatic!

I had just finished being flabbergasted that Trista actually dumped Charlie for Ryan when this story came to me in a flash. I couldn't help but wonder what really happened when the cameras stopped rolling. What if the Bachelor wasn't what he seemed? What would they do with a contestant with an A-cup bra size?

I saw Bridget as the anti-contestant. And since I have always loved the boss/secretary relationship—I'm a longtime fan of Josh and Donna on the *West Wing*—adding Richard as the demanding boss seemed like a perfect recipe for love, some fun and a lot of chaos.

I hope you enjoy this journey into my very warped, highly dramatic and hopefully very entertaining version of reality TV.

I do love to hear from readers. Come visit me at www.stephaniedoyle.net.

Happy reading,

Stephanie Doyle

"There's only one thing to do. Trick him."

This caught Bridget's attention. "What do you mean?"

"Pretend you need him to kiss you for some other reason," Raquel said. "Like you've got a piece of gum stuck on your back tooth and you need him to get it…. Only with his tongue."

The concept had merit—the kissing part, not the gum part. But… "I don't know," Bridget hedged. "You don't think it's a little obvious? I would like to think that Richard and I were more mature than that."

Of course, Richard was oblivious to her feelings, which were apparently pretty obvious to the world. She wouldn't share them with him verbally because she was a scaredy-cat. The two of them basically were afraid of their respective families. Richard drew comic strips for entertainment.

So maybe they were not the two most mature people in the city.

"Trick him," Raquel repeated firmly.

Trick him, Bridget repeated silently. It might just work. Wow, she truly was becoming an evil seductress. All she had to do was sleep with her sister's husband or abscond with someone else's baby, claiming it was hers and it would pretty much be a done deal.

Richard wasn't going to know what hit him….

Who Wants To Marry a Heartthrob?

Stephanie Doyle

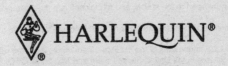

HARLEQUIN®

TORONTO • NEW YORK • LONDON
AMSTERDAM • PARIS • SYDNEY • HAMBURG
STOCKHOLM • ATHENS • TOKYO • MILAN • MADRID
PRAGUE • WARSAW • BUDAPEST • AUCKLAND

ISBN 0-373-44197-5

WHO WANTS TO MARRY A HEARTTHROB?

This edition published by arrangement with Harlequin Books S.A.

® and TM are trademarks of the publisher. Trademarks indicated with ® are registered in the United States Patent and Trademark Office, the Canadian Trade Marks Office and in other countries.

www.eHarlequin.com

Printed in U.S.A.

ABOUT THE AUTHOR

Stephanie Doyle began her writing career in eighth grade when she was given an assignment to write in a journal every day. Her own life being routine, she used the opportunity to write her own sequel to the *Star Wars* movies. One hundred and six handwritten pages later, she discovered her lifelong dream—to be a writer. Currently, Stephanie resides in South Jersey with her cat, Alexandria Hamilton Doyle. Single, she still waits for Mr. Right to sweep her off her feet. She vows that whoever he is, he'll decorate the cover of at least one of her books.

Books by Stephanie Doyle

HARLEQUIN FLIPSIDE
2—ONE TRUE LOVE?

HARLEQUIN DUETS
65—DOWN-HOME DIVA
88—BAILY'S IRISH DREAM

SILHOUETTE INTIMATE MOMENTS
792—UNDISCOVERED HERO

For my brother, Chris. The funniest person I know.

1

"HOUSTON, we have a problem."

"Huh?"

"We have a problem," Bridget Connor repeated, although she didn't know why she bothered. Her employer clearly was not listening. Right now his gaze was pinned on fourteen gorgeous women, each dressed more scantily than the next. Bridget had never seen so much Spandex in one sitting in her life. And she wondered about the engineering of some of the clothes that managed to hold certain body parts in place when it seemed as if the slightest shift might give away the farm, so to speak.

Not that her employer was waiting for a quick flash. Or maybe he was—he was a man after all. But he wasn't ogling the women with the same intent that some of the other men in the room had. No, Richard Wells's priority wasn't sex right now.

It was money.

He turned his head and she could see him squint in her direction. Squinting was Richard's universal sign for "Huh?" After three years of working for him, she was an expert on all of his subtle little expressions.

"Did you say something?" he asked.

"Yep."

"Something about a problem," he recalled. "In Houston?"

"No, here in New York."

He looked confused. "Then why did you say Houston?"

"It's an expression. Work with me, Richard." Then she reminded herself that she needed to be patient with him tonight. Not that it didn't require a great deal of patience to work with the moody ad executive on a normal day, but tonight was different. His focus was solely on the event that was to take place within the next half hour. Nothing short of a nuclear explosion would distract him from that.

"What is it?" he snapped impatiently.

She considered him while he continued to study the room. "You have no intention of listening to a word I say, do you?"

When he turned back to her, he was squinting again.

"I don't have time for problems," he announced.

"I can see that, but you do. Have a problem, that is."

He shook his head as if to deny her words. "What could possibly go wrong? The camera crew is here, the women are here—well, most of them anyway—and my heartthrob is most definitely here." Richard pointed to the man standing by himself, away from the women. Brock Brickman was broad, blond, buffed and the perfect choice for Breathe Better Mouthwash's newly sponsored show—*Who Wants To Marry a Heartthrob?*

"It's about one of the girls," Bridget tried.

Distracted, Richard looked over his shoulder and spotted two men in suits walking through the entryway into the large living room, which had been temporarily transformed into a television set. Don and Dan Meadle were the co-CEOs and owners of Breathe Better Mouthwash. They also happened to be twins, which never failed to amuse Richard and cause him to silently mock the parents who had named them. Obviously, they were here to check up on the project, but he refused to be nervous. Everything was on schedule for his advertising masterpiece.

Who Wants To Marry a Heartthrob? a reality dating show set in New York, was going to put the burgeoning mouthwash company on the map. Two live group shows, four taped individual dates and two romantic weekend getaways, also taped and edited for maximum dramatic effect, would feature exclusively the mouthwash commercials that he had created.

The entire package had been Richard's concept. Once he had found a cable channel that would support the dating show over the course of eight weeks, his vision had become a reality. Now it was time for the show to air and his nerves were being put to the test, although there was absolutely no reason for it, he assured himself. He had left no stone unturned.

The first piece of the puzzle had been finding the location. He and Bridget had searched the summer play area of New York's wealthy, South Hampton, for days. Then they had stumbled on a house that was both markedly luxurious and effortlessly romantic.

The sprawling Victorian sat on an inlet of Long Island Sound. Done in white both inside and out, except for the hints of color strategically added throughout, it lent itself to a summer dream. A covered pool took up space on the green lawn that extended toward the water. And in back of the house there was a massive patio, complete with a hot tub and porch swing. It was a heartthrob's ultimate bait.

The season was right. It was late fall, a little chilly perhaps, but the summer season was over and most of the tourists were gone. This would allow them more flexibility to get the shots on the beach and in the restaurants that they wanted for the four hour-long dates that would be aired individually.

That's right, Richard thought. Not one stone. He had handpicked each of the fifteen women as well as the heartthrob. Every detail of the show was in his control. Nothing escaped his notice. Not Brock's cologne, not the host's tie, not the wardrobe of the ladies. Nothing.

He was investing everything he had into this ad campaign. If it was successful—and it would be because the idea was genius—the Breathe Better Mouthwash executives would have no choice but to follow him when he branched out and opened his own agency. He'd worked for this night for years and success, real success, which to date had been an elusive lady, was within his grasp.

Unfortunately, it was usually moments like this when he thought he was so close to something that nothing could go wrong—that it all went wrong. He need only reflect on that last week before he was to have graduated from Yale to get a reminder of that particularly painful lesson.

"They're here," Richard announced ominously, his chin lifting slightly in the direction of the twins.

Bridget turned and glanced at the two men who were standing off to the side observing the spectacle that was a live television show.

"This is it," Richard told her somewhat fatalistically, feeling his heart beat hard against his rib cage and his palms beginning to sweat. For the most part he wouldn't have considered himself a nervous man, but right now it felt as if his whole life was coming down to this one crucial moment. He glanced at Bridget, grateful for her presence. Not only did he know that he had her support throughout this endeavor, but he also knew that she would cover his tracks if he needed to leave the room real quick to puke. "If this works— And it is going to work, right? We both agree it couldn't fail. Right?"

"Right."

"You're only saying that because you know that's what I want to hear, aren't you," he accused her.

"Right."

He could live with that.

"This will be the big one. The one I've been looking for. The one that is going to free me and my creative genius from the death grip of the V.I.P. Advertising Agency."

Bridget rolled her eyes.

"I saw you do that."

"You're so dramatic," she said. "You've been looking for the 'one' for years now. And V.I.P. doesn't have you in a death grip. They pay you really well. That's why you stay with them."

"It's just that I have a loft in Soho. You know what I pay in rent. I can't quit and start my own agency until I'm positive, absolutely sure, that one of these big companies is going to follow me. But this is it. I can smell it."

"You don't think that's the mouthwash?"

Richard took his eyes off the two executives and focused them on his assistant again. Her lips were turned up in that soft smile that she was famous for. *Subtlety*, he thought, *thy name is Bridget*.

It was there in the way she pulled her midnight hair back into a tight bun, the way she always wore stark black clothes and the way she always maintained a sense of calm even in the face of chaos—as she was doing now. He couldn't help but envy her that serenity.

"You know this night is about your future, too," he told her. "Didn't I promise you I would make you vice president?"

"Ooh. Vice president of a two-person company. A staggering promotion," she quipped. But the truth was she knew that following Richard to his own company was the career break she'd been looking for since she'd graduated college and ended up in the assistant pool at V.I.P. It did occur to her that he'd never really asked her if she was willing to quit V.I.P. and join him in his endeavors. He'd just assumed she would.

He was right of course, but still...a girl liked to be asked.

"Don't you want me to be successful when I do leave?"

She shrugged. "It's not as important to me. I only have an efficiency in Brooklyn."

He smirked at her then turned his attention back to the scene before him. The women were arranging themselves around the room ready to greet their potential husband and heartthrob. Bridget watched Richard count them and waited for him to notice that something was missing.

Then Buzz, the cameraman/director that Richard had hired, approached the two of them. A mobile camera, one of three that they were using for the show, sat heavily on his thick shoulder. He had thick, salt-and-pepper-colored hair that hung heavily down his back, a bushy beard, several tattoos and Richard could see Buzz's round belly where his T-shirt didn't quite meet the top of his jeans.

Suddenly, Richard was very grateful that this man would always be behind the camera. Buzz was definitely not what America was tuning in to see. Richard quickly checked the living room for mirrors and was satisfied when he saw none.

"We've got a problem," Buzz announced.

"I told you," Bridget sang.

Richard glared her into silence. "I know. There are still only fourteen girls. Where's—" Richard scanned the faces of the women, ticking off in his head each of the candidates "—Bambi?"

"Boob accident," Bridget announced. Both men looked at her. "That's what I was trying to tell you. She just called. Apparently she developed complications after her implant surgery."

"What kind of complications?" Richard asked.

"It seems she might have gone a little overboard, three cup sizes overboard to be exact. Her body couldn't hold them up, and as a result, she threw out her back. She's going to be in traction for the next three weeks."

"Three weeks!"

"Wow," Buzz mumbled. "Must be some pretty big boobs."

Richard instantly calmed down. "Fine, we'll do the show with fourteen women."

"We can't," Buzz complained. "You told me fifteen. I set up everything to work for fifteen. The camera shots, the furniture, the props. If there are only fourteen girls it's not going to look right. The shots won't be even."

"Oh, for Pete's sake, it's only a cable show. At best what we're attempting to do here is a beefed-up, overly dramatic infomercial. We're not talking *Masterpiece Theater*," Richard wailed.

"Fifteen is fifteen. I'm a perfectionist."

"We're going live in, like—" Richard glanced at his watch and immediately freaked "—ten minutes! Ten minutes. I can't find another Bambi in ten minutes! Bridget, tell him I can't find another Bambi in five minutes."

"We're fresh out of Bambis, Buzz," she obliged and tried not to smile for fear it would upset Richard that much more. Not that it wasn't fun to get him riled every once in a while, but tonight really wasn't the time.

Buzz shrugged. "Fine. If that's the way you want it. I'm just saying it's going to look funny."

"What's going to look funny?" Dan, one of the co-CEOs, who had wandered over to their side of the room, asked.

Bridget watched in amazement as Richard instantly smoothed out his frazzled expression. He could go from hysterical lunatic to calm businessman like nobody else she knew. It was all an act, but it was a good one.

"Nothing. Everything is fine. "

Don joined them and pointed to Buzz. "He said that it

was going to look funny. We don't want funny. We're not paying for funny. You said everything would be perfect."

"And it will be," Richard insisted to the two men.

"Not with fourteen girls," Buzz muttered.

Richard glared at the cameraman ferociously. "I'll get a girl," he announced.

Dan, Don and Buzz all looked at Richard expectantly.

"I'll get a girl," he repeated. This time with conviction.

Satisfied, Buzz wandered off and so did the executives.

"Great," Richard snapped once everyone was out of earshot. "Buzz, the biker cameraman is really a junior Steven Spielberg in training."

"You did insist on the best," Bridget reminded him.

"I need you to be on my side right now."

She snorted. "That should be in my job description. Filing, message taking, errand running and permanently being on your side."

"You mean it isn't? Add that to your job description as my VP."

"What do you need me to do?"

"Find a girl," he ordered her sounding somewhat desperate.

She laughed. "Where am I going to find a sane single woman who is willing to go on a television game show to win a husband in less than ten minutes?"

"Not just a husband...a heartthrob husband. Brock Brickman *is* America's daytime heartthrob. Clearly you've never seen his work on *The Many Days of Life*."

"Yes, but wasn't he fired?"

"Only a few weeks ago. Which is the only reason he was available to do this show in the first place so let's consider ourselves lucky. He's a semi-star, he's handsome and he's going to pick one of these lucky women to be his wife. One of these lucky *fifteen* women. I just need one more..." Richard's words trailed off even as he surveyed her up and down.

Bridget suddenly got very nervous. Either Richard somehow could see through her dark silk blouse and was checking her out—not likely—or she was being sized up as a piece of meat. A sacrificial piece of meat.

She isn't Bambi, he concluded silently. She didn't have the flowing blond hair, the blue eyes or the body. Bridget more or less resembled a modern-day Audrey Hepburn in *Funny Face*...before the transformation.

She had little to no shape. Her golden-brown eyes, probably her best feature, were covered by thick, dark glasses that he knew she thought were chic, but that actually took up too much space on her face. No doubt her soft pale skin tone would translate as pasty on camera, but he was a desperate man. They could always add a lot of makeup.

"Richard," Bridget growled. "Why are you looking at me like I'm steak and you are a hungry dog?"

"You're single."

"Oh, no," she protested. "No way. Not me."

"Bridge, I'm desperate. You heard Dan. He said no funny."

"That was Don."

"Whatever. I need you."

"If you think I would go on a television show to get a husband... If you think I would go on a television show for any reason, you are out of your mind. You know how I hate the spotlight."

"But this is our future, Bridge!"

Their future. Her heart skipped a beat at his words. She wasn't sure exactly why. Possibly because she had a very real fear she was about to wet her pants. "I'm not going on TV."

"Fine. Don't do this. Don't make this sacrifice. Really, I don't know what I was thinking. I mean, hey, you're happy just being my assistant, right? The idea of running an advertising company alongside me isn't that important to you, is it?"

Bridget stood firm in the face of his guilt-mixed-with-bribery tactic. He was deluding himself if he thought for a moment that she was going to fall for it. She was way too skilled with this tactic to even flinch.

"Okay, I *do* know what I was thinking," he said answering his own question. "I was thinking that you could, for the sake of Buzz's desire to be a perfectionist, Dan's—"

"Don's."

"—Don's desire that absolutely nothing go wrong on this million-dollar ad campaign and, of course, my desire that this show put Breathe Better Mouthwash on every grocery and drugstore shelf in America, thus securing my position as New York's most creative and most successful advertising force, sit in one of those chairs for one hour and look at Brock as if he makes your mouth water! That's it. That is all that I am asking." Richard inhaled deeply, then added, "It's not like you're going to make the first cut."

Why that statement, of all things, should sting, she couldn't say. But she could feel her bottom lip puff out slightly in what she feared was a sulky pout. Bridget didn't do the sulky pout well. Usually, she ended up looking as though her lower lip had been stung by a bee. "And why not?"

"Look at you," Richard said, pointing at her chest. "Now look at them."

Bridget scanned the room of women all working on poses that showed off their...posture...in the best possible light.

"All right," Bridget conceded. "I get your point. Maybe I don't have the figure of Pamela Anderson, but that doesn't mean that Brock might not see my inner beauty."

"Okay," Richard said, using his hands on her shoulders

to spin her and point her in the direction of Brock. "Now, look at him."

Brock currently was trying to check out his reflection in one of the elegant silver pitchers sitting on one of the marble-top tables that lined the foyer of the house. Bridget couldn't imagine that the distorted image satisfied his vanity.

"Hey, do I have something in my teeth?" Brock asked one of the cameramen.

Richard turned Bridget back around to face him. "Please, Bridge. I know you hate the spotlight. But you won't even know the cameras are there. These guys are professionals. You'll sit in one of the chairs, balancing out the shot for Buzz, maybe say hello and goodbye to Brock. He'll pick eight girls, none of whom will be you, and bang! You're back to being my assistant."

"Oh, joy!" she exclaimed with mock enthusiasm. "You mean after being rejected and humiliated on network television, I get to go *back* to being your assistant."

"It's not network, sweetheart, it's cable."

She crossed her arms over her chest and huffed.

"Please," he cajoled, and she could hear him struggling to muster actual sincerity. She hated when he did that. It always weakened her.

"You're my best friend. You're going to be my future business partner," he added. "And friends and partners are supposed to be there for each other, aren't they?"

"What a load of crap," she groaned. Internally though, she felt herself caving.

"No, really, it's true. I read it in a magazine."

"Richard," she pleaded, giving it one last shot. "Don't make me do this."

Damn, he thought. He was beginning to buckle. He hadn't lied when he'd said she was his best friend. His only friend, if truth were told. He'd spent so much of his energy focused on this one goal of getting to the top that he hadn't left a lot of room in his life for family, lovers or even friends. He was pretty sure that Bridget only hung around because of his promise to promote her. Still, she stayed with him and he didn't want to do anything to jeopardize that. But he couldn't blow this opportunity, either. He was *so* close to having everything.

Which meant it was time to bring out the trump card.

"I didn't want to have to do this, Bridge..."

Her eyes narrowed as she tried to read his thoughts. "Oh, no, you wouldn't..."

"Did I mention that I'm desperate?"

"You are a cad," she accused him, sensing the type of blackmail he was about to inflict upon her.

"Did I or did I not attend your sister's wedding with you?"

"Yes," she muttered through gritted teeth knowing where the rest of this conversation was going.

"Did I or did I not pretend to be your loving boyfriend just to get your parents off your back about marriage?"

"Yes," she mumbled.

"And did I or did I not dance with your aunt Edna?"

"Hey," Bridget countered. "Nobody said you had to dance with Aunt Edna."

"But I did it anyway. Danced with her and told her how much I was in love with you. How you were the woman of my dreams and that someday I would win you over and convince you to be my wife. And how many times has your mother tried to fix you up with a blind date since then?"

"None."

"None. One hour. In one of those nice, white, over-stuffed chairs. 'Hello, Brock. Goodbye, Brock.' That's all I'm asking."

Bridget closed her eyes in defeat.

"And maybe if you could summon up a tear or two when he rejects you," Richard added, but quickly shut his mouth when she glared at him.

Her shoulders slumped and she sighed in resignation. It was no use. There was no way she could refuse him. Not after what he had done for her. When she'd gotten the invitation to her sister's wedding with the "and guest" printed on the envelope, she'd almost considered not even attending. If not for the fact that she was in the wedding party, she might have called in sick. But she hadn't wanted to give her family the satisfaction of knowing that she wasn't seeing someone.

Heck, the truth was she rarely was seeing anyone. It was sort of a theme she'd established in high school. Her beautiful sisters got the guys. Bridget...didn't. It had always been that simple.

With the wedding looming, and a very real fear that her mother would attempt to set her up with a date for the event, Bridget got desperate. Her mother didn't have the best taste when it came to picking out dates. They were always either the nephew of a friend's friend—desperately lonely and still living with his mother—or some recent divorcé who was looking to get back in the game. It was sad to acknowledge that her mother didn't really have much faith that Bridget could attract any other sort of man.

So she'd decided the answer to her problem was to take a date home to prove that she was all grown up and capable of attracting a successful, interesting man. Since a man was a mark of success in the Connor household, it was only logical that Bridget bring home the most successful man she knew.

She ended up being turned down by a bagman on the street before she resorted to asking Richard.

He said yes. And something happened that night. He stood by her side the entire evening—well, except for the Aunt Edna tango. Even when her younger sisters tried to lure him onto the dance floor, he resisted. He danced every dance with her, held her tightly in his arms and whispered jokes into her ear so that she would smile in the face of such familial scrutiny. He was sweet, caring, funny and he made her feel like the only woman alive. Most importantly, he saved her from the final humiliation of having to stand in front of the room and not catch the bouquet.

He'd been her hero that night.

And because of it, something had changed between them. She didn't really have a name for it. Lately, she found herself looking at him differently. It was suddenly easier to see beyond the moody genius with the colossal ego and ridiculous demands to the considerate guy hidden beneath. She didn't mind the long hours or the occasional working weekend. And when he ordered in dinner for them and they talked late into the night, it felt...nice. Even a little warm and fuzzy.

A total turnaround from the beginning of their relationship. There had been no warm and fuzzy feelings when they'd started working together. He'd been rude, arrogant and impossible to deal with. Only the fact that she'd managed to match him in wits kept her coming back for more. She also admired his ambition. She'd known even then that if she stuck with him, he could take her as far as she wanted to go in advertising. She didn't have his creativity, but she made up for it with business savvy. Together, they were an unstoppable team at V.I.P.

Since the wedding, she had been wondering what was behind his unflappable drive. Why did he need to work so hard to get to the top? What was he trying to prove and to whom? The wedding had opened her eyes to Richard the man, rather than Richard the employer, adversary and sometimes friend.

She wasn't exactly sure that she liked having her eyes opened. In fact, she was sort of hoping that they would close again real soon. Because one thing was for certain, under no circumstances would she do something so ridiculously cliché as falling for the boss.

Not her.

No way.

Wasn't going to happen.

Except that now, every time he barked an order, she remembered how he'd gotten her the last piece of dark chocolate off the dessert tray. Every time he crashed after he convinced himself that his storyboards were horrible—which they never were—she found herself wanting to pat his head and tell him that everything was going to be all right. And every time he raised his arms in victory and called her into his office so that she could tell him what a genius he was, she remembered how he'd put all that ego aside and made her the focus for one night.

He'd told her parents how amazing her work was and how, when he did leave to start his own ad agency, she was the only one he wanted to come with him. He'd said that he couldn't succeed without her.

And he'd meant it. The bastard!

One lousy night and suddenly she found herself doing the strangest things, like fussing with her appearance. Something she *never* did. Her sisters had taught her at a very early age that she was never going to be as pretty as they were so there was really no point in trying. Bridget agreed. In fact, she'd gone so far as to rebel against makeup, styling products and all beauty accoutrements.

She preferred looking like herself and not some made-up version of herself with too much eye shadow. And in doing so, she felt that she was making a personal stand for inner beauty in women everywhere.

Not to mention it saving her a lot of money.

Until now. These days she wore perfume to the office and tried to style her long, straight hair rather than wearing it in a bun every day. Not that Richard had noticed any of it. Heck, he didn't even think she would make the cut on his stupid show.

Wouldn't that show him if she did make the cut? What would he think then?

The fact that she shouldn't care so much what he thought didn't enter into Bridget's thought process at the moment. Instead she realized that making it to the second round of his stupid show might just prove to him and the world that she was, in fact, a woman.

A desirable woman, if not a spectacularly beautiful one.

Bridget's mind raced with the possibilities. If she could somehow manage to get close to Brock and dazzle him with her keen wit and natural charm, maybe she could convince him to keep her around for a while. Maybe he might actually fall for her and then Richard would be forced to acknowledge that it was possible for other men to find her attractive.

The seeds of a plan sprung deep in her cortex. All she had to do was attract Brock's attention.

Bridget turned her gaze to where he stood amongst five of the bevy of beauties. He was flexing his bicep. They giggled, he smiled, and Bridget wanted to puke. Okay, maybe he wasn't her type. Still, all she had to do was get close enough to talk with him, maybe make him laugh, and she might have a shot.

If that didn't work, she could always try bribing him. It

would be worth anything, if for no other reason than to see Richard eat his words.

"I'll do it," she finally announced.

"Really?" he asked, clearly astonished. "I thought you were going to make me do a lot more begging and pleading. All of which, I have to admit, I was willing to do."

"Not so fast," she said. "My surrender comes at a price. There is a condition."

"Damn, I knew that was too easy," he cursed under his breath. "Okay, let me have it. What do you want?"

"Christmas is coming up in a few months..."

"Oh, no."

"How many minutes before we go live?"

Her smile was sweet, albeit sinful, and his eyes narrowed as he pantomimed rolling up his sleeves. It's not as if he didn't know who he was messing with when he began this particular game. He knew exactly what she was playing for, and considering the stakes, he was willing to negotiate. "One day."

"Two."

"A day and a half."

"Christmas Eve dinner, Midnight Mass and brunch the following morning, all in the presence of my family."

She was going for the gusto. But so was he. "Fine."

"And you have to buy me a present."

"Evil," he whispered.

"It's a little game I like to play called hardball, Richard. You should know it, you're the one who taught me how to play."

"Agreed. Now, let's try and do something with you." Richard scanned the contestants. He remembered from their résumés that one of them was a makeup artist who worked in a salon. "Rachel," he called to one of the girls and motioned her to come over.

A buxom, blue-eyed blonde stood and made her way toward them in a hip-swaying walk that drew the attention of every man in the room. "It's Raquel," the woman said in a perfect imitation of Marilyn Monroe's breathy tones.

"Okay. You're the makeup lady right?"

"I am an artist," she replied, somewhat affronted.

Richard pushed Bridget in front of the woman's face. "Can you do something with her?"

Raquel studied her face. "Well, first we would have to remove all that awful white powder."

"I'm not wearing any makeup," Bridget said.

"Ahh!" the woman gasped clearly horrified at such an announcement.

"Except for my Bobby Brown eyeliner," Bridget conceded. "I mean a girl's got to have something."

"Look," Richard snapped. "We're running out of time. Just do something. Okay?"

"I can try," the woman replied. "I'll need my kit. Come with me."

"Can't you just get it and bring it here?" Bridget asked.

"Oh, I can't carry it. It's way too heavy. My boyfriend...I mean my ex-boyfriend...took it upstairs and left it in one of the bedrooms. Follow me."

"Hurry," Richard urged, only to have Bridget stick her tongue out at him as she walked by. "And while you're at it, take off those glasses, too!"

BRIDGET FOLLOWED the voluptuous Raquel up the stairs, noting the makeup artist's walk as she did. She tried to mimic the hip-swaying action, but each time she thrust her hip out to the left or to the right all she managed to do was throw her body off balance. Tripping her way up the stairs was nowhere near as sexy.

They reached the top hallway and turned into one of the

bedrooms where a full-size trunk sat at the end of the bed. Raquel flipped the latches and opened the lid to reveal a treasure trove of color beneath it.

"Wow," Bridget reacted. She hadn't seen this much makeup in...she'd *never* seen this much makeup.

"I know. I've collected shades from all over the world."

"Really?"

"No, I just think it sounds more exotic when I say that. But they're definitely from all over the tri-state area. New York, New Jersey and Long Island."

Bridget considered informing Raquel that Long Island wasn't a state, but decided they really didn't have enough time. Instead she grabbed a chair from a corner of the room and pulled it close to the trunk. She took off her glasses and tucked them into the pocket of her black capri pants.

"Okay," Bridget said lifting her face. "Have at it. Just don't make me look like a hooker."

Again, Raquel appeared to be offended. "Do I look like a hooker?"

Bridget considered the body-hugging strapless red dress that clung to the woman's figure like plastic wrap. "Uh...no?"

Moments later various brushes were running over her face as Raquel talked. "The truth is you have very smooth skin. If I had more time, and could do something with your hair, and your clothes and your breasts—"

"Hey, no messing with my breasts," Bridget stated. But the idea did have merit. If she could stay on the show for another round, get a little professional help, maybe she could pull an ugly duck–beautiful swan transformation. That would mean Raquel would have to stick around, too. "So, do you think you'll make the first cut?"

"Of course I do."

Bridget envied the woman's confidence.

"What makes you so sure? There are a lot of beautiful women downstairs."

"I gave him a note that said I would be willing to perform multiple sexual acts on his body."

"That's cheating!"

"It is?"

Bridget shook her head trying to understand. "But you don't even know him. And besides that you have a boyfriend."

"Shh," Raquel whispered. "Not so loud. The rules said you weren't supposed to have a boyfriend."

"For a very good reason," Bridget told her. "If Brock picks you, it's to be his wife."

"Oh, silly, that's not what this show is about."

"It's not?"

"No. I mean, of course that's the end result, but really we're all here for very different reasons. I'm here because I want to be a star. Maybe even do a cosmetics commercial one day."

Bridget considered the women downstairs and didn't imagine that their reasons were all that different. Except for hers, of course. Her reasons were perfectly legitimate. She was going to do the show to make her employer—who she secretly feared she was developing feelings for—eat crow for thinking she couldn't make the cut, and to prove to him that she was more than just an assistant. What more noble reasons could there be than that?

"All done," Raquel announced.

Bridget pulled back and took the hand mirror that Raquel handed her. Wow! She looked different. Not hooker-different, either. Raquel had just added subtle shades under her cheekbones, over her eyes and on her lips that seemed to make her features stand out in the best sort of way. And she did it all without adding any more eyeliner.

So much for Bridget's great makeup rebellion. This actually looked good on her.

"You *are* an artist."

"Told you." Raquel closed her case and started for the door. "Come on, we don't want to be late."

Bridget agreed. She reached for the glasses in her pants pocket and put them on.

"Eeek!" Raquel screeched when she saw her. "You can't wear those, you might smudge. Besides that, I don't like to see my work go unnoticed. Call it the creative genius in me."

Great, Bridget thought. Between Buzz, Richard and Raquel this show was going to have more geniuses than it knew what to do with. "But I can't see. Seriously, after ten feet everything blurs."

The blonde held her two hands palms up then shifted them back and forth as if weighing the choices. "Beauty. Sight. Beauty. Sight. Beauty."

"How do you figure that?"

"Silly, beauty always wins."

"Fine," Bridget grumbled and put the glasses back into her pocket. She would just have to try really hard not to squint. She didn't imagine that Brock had a secret desire for squinters.

Carefully, she followed Raquel down the stairs and knew that the foggy blur at the bottom was Richard.

"Hurry," he urged the two women on.

"I can't see," Bridget hissed.

"And I can't hurry in heels," Raquel told him, pouting.

Finally, they made it to the bottom of the stairs. Richard took a hard look at Bridget, and up close, she could see that he nodded in satisfaction. "Okay, now let's get you both on the set."

Buzz directed them where to sit. He picked out a single

hardback chair for Bridget and placed her in it. "Sit up, chin out, boobs...oh. Never mind."

Bridget tried not to take offense. She saw Brock leaning against a wall in the foyer and tried to get his attention. At least she thought it was Brock. It could have been a coat rack for all she knew.

"Okay, this is it," the host announced. "Smile, ladies, and remember you are trying to win the heart of America's daytime heartthrob, so dirty tricks, cat fighting, name calling and tears are all perfectly acceptable. Good luck."

Bridget saw one of the cameramen circle the room bringing the hulking piece of equipment with him. She tried to brace herself for the impact of knowing that in less than five, four, three...seconds, the camera was going to be on her.

She turned her head and saw Richard standing just out of range of the camera with his two thumbs in the air. Or were they two fingers?

Don't think, she told herself. If she began to think she might begin to realize that she was going to be on TV and that might cause her to panic.

Too late.

Breathe, she ordered herself. She was doing this for a reason. She was doing this to prove something to her family, to Richard...maybe even to herself. She could compete for a man's affection with gifts like intelligence and humor and she wasn't completely unworthy of a man's attention. She would show Richard that she could make the cut and then maybe he would stop taking her for granted.

That's right. It wasn't about any hidden feelings she had for him. It certainly wasn't because she wanted to make him jealous. That would be ridiculous. She only wanted him to see how wrong he was about her.

"Hey, can you pull back a little," she heard Richard say

to Buzz, who now had the camera focused on her. "I think she's got something in her nose."

She was an idiot.

2

"So Brock," Chuck, the show's host began, as most hosts do, with a fake smile and an even faker-sounding voice. "Tell us what you are looking for in a woman."

Brock, who sat next to Chuck in the center of a half arc of fawning women, seemed to ponder the question. He rubbed his chin for a moment, turned to the camera that was focused on him and gazed directly into it, as if letting the viewing audience in on his thoughts before he said anything aloud.

"So many things, Chuck," he responded. "I'm not looking for someone who is just hot. You know what I mean?"

"I do, Brock. I do."

Not just hot. Suddenly, Bridget perked up a little. She had to admit she'd been feeling somewhat disenchanted after she'd spent time conversing with the other contestants during the first commercial break. Apparently they were all as equally determined as her to land Brock's affections and at least make the first cut. Only the most pathetic would be getting the boot tonight, and she sensed that most of the women she talked to counted her as being on that list.

Their reasons for wanting to stay did vary. Some wanted to continue because they thought he was a babe. Some because they wanted to be the wife of Dr. Noah Vanderhorn, the legendary thoracic surgeon with a troubled past and a vulnerability for dangerous women, from the daytime television show *The Many Days of Life*. Most of them, however, wanted their own career in daytime television and starring with Brock Brickman, even if it was on a game show, seemed to be the best approach.

When Bridget suggested training as an actress, preparing a headshot and a résumé and going on auditions, they looked at her as if she was crazy. *What did she know about anything?* they asked. She wasn't even showing cleavage.

Well, now she knew that Brock wanted more than just someone who was attractive.

Take that, girls!

"I want someone with a soul, too," he confessed to Chuck.

Soul. Bridget glanced around the room and decided that most of these women had foregone soul for silicon. It was beginning to look as though she had a shot at him after all. She smiled and tried to flutter her eyelashes, but Raquel had gone a little thick on the mascara and they ended up sticking a little.

"Of course, hot doesn't hurt," Brock added, then nudged the host's elbow with his own as if sharing a private joke.

The women, who had been slumping progressively throughout his little speech, suddenly came to life again. Shoulders were thrown back, chins were lifted and hair was flicked. The blonde next to Bridget caught her square in the mouth with a chunk of hair. Bridget turned her head away and the hair was gone, but the taste of hairspray lingered. She tried not to make a horrible scrunch face as she attempted to lick the spray from her teeth.

Please don't let the camera see me doing this.

"WHAT IS that one woman doing?" the Breathe Better Mouthwash executive asked, pointing to the screen.

Richard stood next to Dan or Don—he really needed to learn which one was which—off camera watching the show on a television monitor. He didn't have an answer for the CEO because he really didn't know what Bridget was doing. First, her eyes had started blinking furiously. Now, she was doing something with her face. For a moment, he feared she was having some kind of seizure. He never should have forced her to do this, he realized. Bridget simply wasn't cut out for this kind of attention. If he hadn't known that from his three years of working with her, he'd certainly learned it at her sister's wedding.

Bridget liked to blend. She was the kind of person who was always there, but was never seen. The ultimate assistant: always on hand, but never underfoot. It wasn't until after the wedding that he began to understand where that quality came from.

Four sisters. Each of them more stunning than the next. Each one of them knowing it, too. Bridget was the worst kind of Cinderella in a family like that, situated between the two older and two younger stars, with a mother who prized beauty and landing a prince above smarts and success.

And Bridget had too much pride even to ask for a fairy godmother.

"Can you make her stop doing that?" Don or Dan asked.

Richard took his eyes away from the monitor and moved back toward the living room, standing just behind Pete, one of the cameramen. At least Bridget seemed to have cleared up her facial tic and once again was focused intently on Brock.

In this particular group of women, she stood out simply because she was so unremarkable. A bubble of annoyance gurgled in his gut and he suddenly had an irrational desire to walk onto the set, grab her arm and get her the hell out of there.

He didn't want anyone sitting at home watching this show to wonder what she was doing on TV with those other gorgeous women. He didn't want anyone thinking that she was desperate. She wasn't. She was doing him a favor. And in some ways, she was one of the most beautiful women he knew.

Not to mention the kind of guts it took to sit alongside a panel of women who looked like that. But the audience couldn't see guts.

This was his fault. He'd made her do this and now he regretted it. And the worst part was yet to come. Brock still had to reject her on television in front of everyone. The reality of that was sinking in now that the moment was fast approaching. Suddenly anxious, Richard wondered if she would ever forgive him for this...and why it mattered so much to him if she didn't.

"Okay, let's hear from the ladies," Chuck decided, still oozing his unique charm. "Tell me what you're looking for in a potential mate. Raquel."

"I'm looking for someone just like Brick Brockman."

"You mean Brock Brickman," the host corrected her quickly.

"That's right." She smiled and pulled her shoulders together a bit more to enhance her cleavage. "Brick Brockman. He's my ideal man."

"Okay, moving right along. You, Jenna?"

A sultry brunette with impossibly blue eyes stood and drew all eyes to her. Bridget had already determined that this woman was no fool. She had a goal, and Bridget assessed that Jenna would be undaunted in the pursuit of that goal. This woman was going to marry Brock or land a role in a soap opera.

Whichever came first.

She looked at Brock then shifted her head slightly, no doubt to give her best side to the camera, and told everyone in clear strong tones, "I'm looking for someone who completes me. Someone who fills my heart and is filled in return by all the love I have to give. I don't want just a husband, but a life mate. A partner. Someone I can share my innermost feelings with, not to mention my innermost...desires." She sat down again with a flick of her hair and a sultry glance that might have been aimed at Brock, or at the camera behind him.

Wow. That was some speech, Bridget silently applauded. She only hoped she didn't have to follow that.

"And Bridget, tell us what are the pieces that make up your Mr. Perfect?"

There were times, she decided, that life could be entirely unfair.

"Uh...well, he...should...uh...I suppose I'm looking for..." The camera guy zoomed in on her and the blinking light above it forced her to turn her eyes away. The light also didn't help with her stuttering.

"Ah," Chuck extolled. "I see we have a shy one here. Please, don't be scared. All of America wants to know what it is you're looking for in a man."

All of America. Bridget gulped. "I guess what I'm really searching for is..."

"I'm sorry." Chuck stopped her with a raised hand and turned his back on her to speak directly to the camera. "But we're out of time."

"Why does that not surprise me," she muttered under her breath.

"This is the part of the show where Brock must retire to his solitary space. In that space he will have to ask himself 'Is she the right one for me?' Fifteen women will receive an invitation, and in that invitation there will be either a green card or a red card. Green means she gets to go on to the next show to see if she can win the heart of our heartthrob. Red means that life has chosen another course for her. Tonight only eight cards will be green. We'll be right back to watch our ladies open their invitations. As always *Who Wants To Marry a Heartthrob?* is brought to you by Breathe Better Mouthwash, the mouthwash choice of singles. Because at those critical moments it's important to have good breath. Your *future* could depend on it."

Bridget winced at the phrase that Richard had finally decided on as the tag line for the campaign.

Breathe Better Mouthwash—because your future could depend on it.

She'd told him it was too dramatic. But with Chuck saying it as if mouthwash were a life-or-death decision, she thought it superceded dramatic and launched directly into the melodramatic. *Typical Richard,* she thought to herself. Always pushing. Always going over the top.

The red lights on top of the cameras abruptly went dark and Bridget breathed a sigh of relief. During each of the intermissions some of the women had had a chance to speak with Brock one-on-one. Getting close to him, however, meant running a gauntlet of pointed elbows and spiky heels.

Fortunately, Bridget had an edge over the crowd since she wasn't as afraid of bruising as some of the other women were. She had actually made it to his side during the last commercial, but had only managed, "Hi, my name is..." before someone—her money was on Jenna—had knocked her out of the way. Now would be her last chance to impress him if she had any hope of getting a green invitation.

She stood up, scanned the room for Brock and saw him being whisked away by Chuck down a hallway that led to one of the studies in the back of the house. She was about to follow in pursuit when, of all people, Richard moved in front of her path.

"Okay, I'll say it. I was wrong and you were right. I never should have made you do this. I'm sorry."

She knew she should have been thrilled with such a statement, especially coming from someone who hoarded apologies the way Scrooge hoarded coal on Christmas Eve. But hearing this from Richard at this particular moment wasn't good news. No doubt after watching her on the monitor, it was obvious that she didn't belong with the others. But she wasn't going to let the fear that she might have made a fool out of herself on television stop her from getting what she wanted.

And what she wanted was Richard. *No, no, no,* she thought, shaking that idea completely out of her head. She wanted Brock. Well, not really Brock. Just another night with Brock to teach Richard a lesson.

"Richard, move out of the way." Bridget attempted to move around him, but he stepped with her, continuing to block her path. And he was big. Sometimes she forgot how tall he was, but when she stood toe-to-toe with him she barely reached his chin. It was the lean, easy quality about him that made her forget sometimes that he was, in fact, a lot of man.

"No. I guilted you into it. I forced you in front of a camera, made you put on all that makeup, which I know goes against your whole inner-beauty-motto thing—although I have to say, it really does look nice on you—and now I've set you up for this failure."

His last item had her stopping in her tracks. "Failure?"

"I know and I'm sorry. You're going to have to open that stupid invitation, get that red card. It's going to be horrible. But listen, I talked to Buzz and I specifically told him to keep you off camera as much as possible. It will be like the Oscars. As soon as he sees red, he'll move the camera off you."

It was stupid and not like her at all, but she actually felt tears welling up in her eyes. His lack of faith in her, well, womanhood, was crushing. Despite the makeup, despite taking off her glasses and despite her attempt at eye fluttering, he didn't even consider the possibility that Brock might pick her. All he saw was a failure.

"I'm really sorry, Bridge."

"Me, too," she mumbled trying to contain an odd feeling of loss, as though she'd had something within her reach, but now it was fading from sight. Forcefully, she stopped the tears. The last thing she needed to do was actually cry and ruin Raquel's artfully applied mascara.

"And if it means anything, I would have picked you."

She lifted her face and met his hazel-green gaze. "You're just saying that to make me feel better."

He cupped her face in his hands and leaned down to give her a quick kiss on the nose. "Look into my eyes."

"You're not going to hypnotize me, are you?"

"No," he chuckled. "You know when I'm telling the truth. And you know when I'm lying, right?"

She did. She knew everything about him. His favorite foods, his weird allergy to all things sesame and his preference for tea over coffee. She also knew that often when he was in the middle of an important meeting, he was really zoned out creating cartoon characters in his head. Everything.

"Right."

"I'm not lying now. I would pick you. It's as plain as the nose on your face. And by the way, nice job getting rid of that booger."

"It wasn't a booger," she hissed. "It was a piece of lint."

"Whatever. The point is, you're the only woman here I would want to get to know better."

"Really?"

"I would want to know why you wear your hair all back in a bun like that. And I would want to know why you're dressed all in black, and I would want to know why you keep squinting at the camera."

"Because you made me take off my glasses, and I can't see very far," she reminded him.

"Yes, but I wouldn't know that if I had just met you. Brock's a fool. Here he's got the most amazing woman right in front of him, and he doesn't know it."

A reply sprang to her lips, but before Bridget could open her mouth, Buzz interrupted her.

"Yo, chicks! Places."

"Apparently Buzz doesn't understand the basics of political correctness," Richard murmured, turning his attention to the fact that they were about to start broadcasting again. "Go sit down, open your silly invitation and I'll take you out for ice cream afterward."

"Your treat," she insisted. "And I'm ordering extra fudge."

He smiled, bent down to kiss her cheek and headed back to the foyer where the monitor was.

Bridget sat down in the chair that Buzz had picked out for her and girded herself against the rejection that was to come. She smiled at Raquel who gave her a thumbs-up sign, and Bridget mimicked the gesture.

Chuck came back into the room with the fifteen envelopes in his hand. He waited until the cameramen were in place around the room and watched Buzz as he silently counted down to live with his fingers.

As soon as Buzz made a fist, the lights on the camera lit up, and so did Chuck's smile. "Hello everybody, we're back." He turned to Brock who had come into the living room to stand next to him. "Brock, have you made your very difficult decision?"

"I have," he nodded dramatically. He wrapped an arm around the host's shoulders and shook him a bit. "And it was difficult. What man in his right mind could decide between all these lovely ladies? It was almost impossible."

"I understand, Brock. But rest assured that each of the women not selected tonight will receive as a consolation gift a free year's supply of Breathe Better Mouthwash. So you see, there is a light at the end of this particular tunnel."

Brock smiled wistfully. "That does make me feel better."

"Now to the moment we've been waiting for. I have in my hand fifteen invitations, ladies. Please wait until I've distributed them all, then when I give the word, go ahead and open them. Those with a green card will continue on, and those with a red card... Well, at least you'll have fresh breath."

Brock lifted his arm from around Chuck's shoulders, and Chuck moved forward to present each of the invitations to the women. Some women tried to hold them up to the light to see the color of the card within it. Some blew kisses to Brock. Others tried to fan themselves with the invitation in an effort to calm their nerves.

Bridget dropped the invitation in her lap and tried to focus on the hot fudge sundae that she was going to order. She also was thinking that the idea of proving to Richard that there had to be some man out there...somewhere...who might find her desirable still had merit. Why it was important, she wasn't quite willing to deal with, but that it *was* important couldn't be denied.

First she would need to find someone who found her attractive enough to pursue her. Or pretend to pursue her.

Hey, that was an idea. Maybe she could hire an actor.

"Ladies, open your invitations," Chuck announced.

Of course, she wouldn't want an actor who looked like Brock. She would want someone more real looking. The type of man who Richard would believe she could attract. She wondered how much actors charged for a few hours of work.

"Wait, we're missing one."

If Richard and she did manage to steal Breathe Better Mouthwash from V.I.P. and Richard did open up his own ad agency, then no doubt times would be lean for a while until they got the business off the ground. She'd have to be frugal about this.

"I picked eight," Brock said forcibly enough to jar Bridget out of her musings.

Realizing that she actually had forgotten she was on a television show, she glanced around the room to size up the situation. All of the women had their invitations open. Green and red cards abounded. That is, seven green cards and seven red cards. One card was missing.

Hers!

"Oh, I'm sorry. I forgot to open mine," Bridget muttered a little sheepishly digging into her invitation. She pulled the card from the envelope and held it up for the camera to see. There. Green. Just as she expected...

"Green!" she gasped.

"Green!" Richard shouted from off camera.

"Green!" fourteen women screeched simultaneously, turning their heads in unison to see this purported green card.

"Green," Brock confirmed. He turned to Chuck to explain. "She was always making funny faces at me. I like a woman who can make me laugh."

"And there you have it, everyone. Our heartthrob has chosen. Tune in next week to see how this particular plot thickens. Watch as some women will woo, and others will boo-hoo when they get the red card. Next time on *Who Wants To Marry a Heartthrob?* brought to you by Breathe Better Mouthwash, the mouthwash choice of singles. Because your *future* could depend on it."

"And cut," Buzz called. "Let's clean it up, guys."

Richard marched over to where Brock was chatting with Chuck and rudely tapped the actor on the shoulder.

"What in the hell was that?" Richard asked when Brock turned around.

Brock broke out into an all-white-tooth grin. "Great show, huh? Hey, man, thanks again for this opportunity. It's only been a few weeks since I got canned from *The Many Days of Life,* but I'm really starting to worry about my career, you know. Last week at the mall I was only stopped twice for an autograph. Twice," he repeated in low whisper. "That's pathetic. But this is going to put me right back on top. I'm sure of it. *The Many Days of Life* will have to take me back."

"Look at my face," Richard demanded. "Do I look like a man who cares about your career?"

Brock's brow furrowed. "Uh...no?"

"No! I want to know what the hell you were doing picking Bridget?"

Brock glanced over at the assembled green-card ladies who were chatting it up as they drank their celebratory glasses of champagne.

"Which one is Bridget?"

"That one." Richard pointed to Bridget who stood apart from the other seven women still staring at her green card.

"Oh, her. She had a nice smile."

"Yes, I know she has a nice smile, but look at her will you? She doesn't belong on TV."

Brock shrugged. "I don't know. Maybe if she was looking to do some character acting..."

"She doesn't want to act!" Richard shouted, incensed. "She's my assistant. You have to pick someone else."

"Too late for that, Richard," Chuck intervened. "The other women are already gone, and besides it made for great TV having the dark horse pull ahead in the end. She represents the every woman. You watch, the audience will eat her up. She'll be an asset to the show."

Richard wanted to shout again, but there was really no one to shout to. The deed was done and Bridget would be returning for another week. And it was his damn fault. Oh well, he thought. One more week couldn't hurt. By then Brock would come to his senses and Richard would have his Bridget back.

Chuck and Brock left and Richard made his way to where she was still standing in apparent shock, snatching two glasses of celebratory champagne off the table on his way.

He handed her one and she beamed at him.

"Green," she said, showing him the card.

"So I see."

"He picked me."

"Yes, I understand how the game is played."

Bridget sipped her champagne and tried to stifle a giggle. It was entertaining to see Richard so clearly agitated—a predictable state for him when things didn't go according to plan. "Funny, isn't it? Because you seemed so sure that he wasn't going to pick me, then he did pick me."

"Yes, yes," he snapped. "I get it. He picked you. I was wrong."

"Really wrong. Colossally wrong. Napoleon at Waterloo wrong. Britney Spears as a brunette wrong—"

"How long are you going to hold this over my head?" he asked, cutting her off.

"I would say the statute of limitations for mocking runs out in about a year on this one."

Richard groaned. "Fine. Consider this though, getting picked means you have to go back on TV next week. Next week is party night, too. No formal questions, just mingling. And we all know how you love to mingle, Bridge."

She scowled at him. She hated to mingle. In fact, she hated parties, borne from a lifetime of watching her sisters be the life of every one they had ever attended. Since from a very young age she had known she didn't have it in her to be the life of the party, she had decided to go the other way. She hugged walls, watched people and counted away the hours until she could leave and be free of the pressure of being a Connor girl at a party.

"But I'm sure you'll be fine," he recanted.

Richard had watched her face fall and he'd felt a little guilty raining on her parade so quickly. She'd been truly pleased that she had been picked out from among the throng. He didn't want to spoil that. But he also didn't want her getting her hopes up. Next week would be the end of this particular fairy tale. And at the end of the day, he needed his sensible assistant back.

Bridget regarded him as he sipped his champagne.

"This tastes horrible," he noted, putting the glass down.

"It's domestic," she informed him. When he gasped, she reminded him, "Cable, remember. The budget didn't call for foreign. So, let me get this straight. You don't think I stand any chance of getting another green card next week, do you?"

"No."

"You didn't think I had any chance this week."

"No."

"But I did."

"Fluke," he quipped. He didn't want to believe otherwise.

"Really," she mumbled. "Care to place a wager on that?"

"You want to bet me?"

"A bet might make things more interesting."

"What do you want?"

"If I get the green card next week, you agree to go on a vacation with me and my family in the Poconos for an entire weekend."

"Deal. And if I win...you have to clean my loft for a month. Laundry and cooking included."

"Deal," she agreed and stretched out her hand. They shook and the bet was sealed. "That's odd, though, I assumed you would have wanted to get out of Christmas."

"The Christmas thing is only for two days, this is clean underwear for a month," he told her.

That wasn't entirely true. He'd cut his tongue out before he admitted it to her, but the truth was he was glad to have somewhere to go during the holidays. Bridget was his closest friend, and there really wasn't anyone else he would rather spend that time with. Certainly not with his overly stuffy, extraordinarily successful family who would use the holidays to grill him about his net worth, his prospects for the future and his chances of making partner at V.I.P. Not that creating ad campaigns was a job worthy of the Wells name.

No, the next time he saw his family he wanted to present them with his own business. His name on the office door. His company that he would build into a success. Then maybe, just maybe, he would be forgiven for his lifetime of underachievement.

Bridget shrugged at his response and took another sip of her champagne. He was right. It was awful. But it didn't matter. Not tonight. She had been picked above seven other beautiful women. She planned to savor the victory.

Not for too long, though. There was work to be done if she was going to compete seriously in next week's show and she knew just the person to help her.

"Raquel!" Bridget called to the woman standing in the group of seven. Squealing with joy, Raquel bounced her way over to where Bridget and Richard stood.

"Oh, isn't this exciting? Imagine, me on TV two weeks in a row."

"Congratulations," Richard offered her.

"Thank you, but I really had no doubt. But you, Bridget. See what mascara and the right shade of lipstick can do for you?"

"I'm beginning to," she replied. "Listen, Raquel, if it wouldn't be too much trouble, do you think you could help me out for next week? I'm going to need a dress and more makeup and—"

"More makeup?" Richard protested. "What happened to all that stuff about not giving in to society's dictates and taking the inner beauty high ground?"

"You were the one who made me put the makeup on in the first place!"

"That was when I thought it would be just once," he countered. "Twice might compromise your morals."

"Hello," Bridget replied. "One word—television. There are no morals here."

"She's right," Raquel agreed. "And say no more. Raquel to the rescue. Hee, hee, that rhymes."

Neither Richard nor Bridget had the heart to tell her that it really didn't.

"Give me your address and I will pick you up tomorrow. Then we'll go shopping."

"Hey," Richard complained. "Tomorrow is a work day."

"And this is work," Bridget informed him. "I'm doing this for the show and for the client."

"It will be so much fun," Raquel bubbled. "I know just the dress place we should hit first. They have the most marvelous things for women. Even for women without breasts!"

"I have breasts," Bridget grumbled.

"If you insist."

"Sounds to me like a lot of effort for nothing." This came from Jenna who had strolled over to their group during the conversation. "You don't actually think a new dress is going to help you, do you dear?"

Bridget had to hand it to the woman, she played the catty bitch better than anyone on daytime television she'd ever seen. As a reply, she merely held up her card. "Green."

Jenna smiled, displaying all of her white, perfectly formed teeth. "This week."

She turned to Richard and moved up against him, definitively invading his personal space. "It's good to see you again, Richard. I never really got a chance to tell you how much I enjoyed dinner with you the other evening."

"Uh..." he stuttered. "Sure. Dinner. It was nice."

Bridget watched the scene in complete fascination. She wasn't jealous. Richard had dated several women throughout the three years she'd known him, none of whom had ever exceeded his four-date limit. He had several goals in life, but as far as she knew establishing a long-term relationship wasn't one of them. Which was really one more reason why any nebulous and burgeoning feelings she might have for him were ludicrous. She was the ultimate long-term relationship girl. At least, she'd always thought she would be. Those kinds of thoughts, however, were for another time.

For now, Bridget needed to concentrate on Jenna. Maybe she could learn something from her. Currently, she was wielding seduction skills the way a samurai wielded a sword. Bridget watched how Jenna slid her hand up the front of Richard's suit coat. The way she leaned into his body without actually touching him. The way she tilted her neck at just the right angle to give a man a few ideas.

And Richard, Bridget did not doubt, was a man who could quickly get ideas.

Jenna made it all seem so effortless.

"We'll have to do it again sometime," she purred, then chuckled. "That is, if Brock doesn't pick me to be his wife."

"Sure," Richard concurred.

"Ladies. Until next week." She turned and sauntered away and again Bridget couldn't help but be impressed by how she managed to walk on those heels. It was something Bridget was going to have to practice. Right after she bought a pair of shoes with heels.

For effect however, she turned to glare at Richard. She wasn't really angry with him, but there was no point in letting him off the hook that easy.

"What?" he asked in reference to her glare. "I was interviewing her."

The glare continued.

"Hey, that's not fair," he replied to her silent accusation.

Her eyes only narrowed farther.

"Okay, maybe it is fair, but nothing happened. She's trying to mess with you. Don't let her get to you."

"I don't plan to," Bridget assured him. "Now, I believe someone promised me ice cream."

"That was for when you lost," he said. "You won, which means you treat."

Bridget scowled but figured that was only fair. "Want to come along, Raquel?"

"And do what?"

"Eat ice cream," Bridget explained although she was pretty sure that had been obvious given the fact that they were going out for ice cream.

"Ice cream? You mean that stuff with all the fat and sugar and calories in it?"

"Yep, that about sums up ice cream."

"I couldn't possibly."

But Bridget could see she was tempted. "When was the last time you had ice cream?"

"I don't remember," Raquel whispered as if she were committing some sin by even considering it.

"It's really good."

"I suppose, maybe, they have a low-fat variety?"

"Nope. Not this place. All fat and hot fudge."

"And sprinkles," Richard added.

"Sprinkles," Raquel repeated as if she were saying *diamonds* instead.

"My treat."

"Okay, but I want to state for the record that I agreed under stress," Raquel proclaimed and marched off in search of her coat.

Richard considered that. "I think she meant duress."

Bridget smiled. Her new friend might not be the brightest, but she was an artist, and Bridget was planning on putting her face, hair and body safely in this woman's hands.

She only hoped that Raquel was up to the challenge.

3

"YOU HAVE to come out," Raquel explained patiently. "Or how can I possibly see what the dress looks like on you?"

"Trust me. It's no good," Bridget said from behind the dressing-room curtain.

"That's what you've said about every one so far."

"Because they have all been no good." Bridget looked in the mirror and winced. This dress was a clingy, strapless silk number done in a deep purple that fell to just below her butt. Every time she tried to pull it down to completely cover her bottom one of her breasts popped free.

Suddenly, the curtain was thrust aside and Bridget tried to cover her exposed breast with her hands.

"No," Raquel determined. "That's not right."

"Thank you," Bridget sighed. "Let's face it. It's hopeless. We're never going to agree. Why can't I just find a nice, simple, black cocktail dress?"

"Because the point of this game is to stand out. We have to be like the peacock and ruffle our feathers."

"What are you wearing?"

"A black cocktail dress," Raquel admitted. "But I am, by my very nature, a peacock."

Having no idea what that meant, Bridget instead glanced down at the one-billionth dress Raquel held in her hands.

"Try this one." Raquel shoved the dress at her, pushed

her back into the dressing room and closed the curtain with a deft motion.

Bridget stared down at the garment and sighed. It was time to face facts. A dress wasn't going to turn her into a beauty. She looked into the mirror and took in her white skin, dark hair, which today she had pulled back into a ponytail, and her sticklike body.

Okay, maybe not sticklike, she decided. She did, in fact, have breasts, just not that much of them. She knew that because they kept popping out of dresses at the most unexpected times.

This dress was red. A vibrant red. A red so bright, she considered putting on sunglasses before trying it on. But she knew if she balked, Raquel would stomp her foot and pout, and for whatever reason, Bridget found herself slightly intimidated by the pout.

So she removed the purple concoction and stepped into the red number. It circled her neck leaving her shoulders and arms bare. It fell to the top of her knees, for which she was truly grateful, and when she turned...

"Something is missing," Bridget announced through the curtain.

Again, it slid open and Raquel stood in the doorway. "What?"

"It's got no back. Go out there and find it for me will you?"

"Silly, it's not supposed to have a back. Now turn around and let me see the front."

Bridget did as instructed and Raquel oohed. "You're oohing. Don't ooh. This is not an ooh dress. It's got no back."

"Just look at yourself, will you?" Raquel moved out of the way and Bridget left the tiny dressing area. Three full-length mirrors stood at the end of the tiny dressing-room hallway and Bridget walked toward them, wondering the whole time who the girl in the red dress was. It shimmered as she moved. Instead of making her seem too pale, it made her skin glow. The neckline plunged, but the gathered material sort of left the contents of her chest a mystery and when she turned...

"Ooh," Bridget moaned.

"See."

The dress did scoop dramatically, barely covering the small of her back, but the effect was...not so bad. Who knew she had such a killer back?

"This one?" she asked Raquel, confirming what she already suspected.

"That one."

Bridget turned and studied herself again. "I'll take it."

"Wonderful," Raquel stated.

"Does this mean we're done?" Bridget asked hopefully. She couldn't remember a day when she'd worked harder, and all they had done so far was shop.

"Don't be silly. Now we need shoes."

Bridget groaned. Shoes. She was never going to make it.

LATER THAT DAY, she limped her way into Richard's office. He looked up from his drafting table and grimaced. "What happened to you?"

"Shoe accident," she muttered. She hung her dress, draped in black plastic, on his coat rack then hobbled her way to the stool positioned on the other side of his drawing table. She climbed up on it and sighed in blessed relief to be off her feet.

"Shoe accident?"

"Yeah, I fell off a pair. You would be amazed at how high those things can actually go."

He chuckled and nodded his head toward the dress. "Is that it?"

"It is."

"Can I see it?"

"No." She wanted it to be a surprise. Raquel had big plans for her including the dress, the sandals they had picked out to go with it that were currently being dyed to match, a new hairstyle and makeup. When all was said and done, Bridget was going to be a new woman and she wanted the effect to be startling.

So startling Richard might feel compelled to walk up to her, proclaim to the world his hidden passion for her—which, in all honesty, she wasn't sure she exactly wanted him to have, but it played much better in her fantasy—and then sweep her off her feet.

At least she hoped he would sweep her off her feet. She really didn't walk so well in the shoes.

"What are you doing?" she wondered aloud, taking a peek at his drawing.

He glanced around to make sure no one was passing by his office door then answered, "Stuff."

"Stuff" for Richard meant non-work-related comic-strip stuff. Bridget never understood why he got so anxious about people uncovering his big dark secret. The great mystery was that the creative force behind most of V.I.P.'s successful ad campaigns was also a truly gifted cartoonist.

Whenever she asked him when he'd begun drawing comics, he'd shrug and mumble something about being a kid. Then invariably he would try to pretend it meant nothing to him. He would demean it by calling it a hobby. Or recreational drawing. Her favorite was when he referred to it as his creative Drano. Whenever the ideas stopped flowing for a product, he invariably turned back to the strip to get the creative juices moving.

The first time she saw one of his strips, she had immediately fallen in love with his talent. For months afterward she had begged him to submit the strip to a paper, a magazine, someone who could render a professional judgment. But he refused. Every once in a while, she would broach the subject again, but invariably he would balk.

Comic strips weren't serious; advertising was serious, he would tell her.

The last time he'd said that she'd pointed out that writing an ad for a company called Breathe Better Mouthwash was not exactly what she would call serious. But he hadn't budged.

"Let me see this one," Bridget said.

He pushed the white paper filled with the neatly arranged boxes over the top of the two-sided desk and let her study it.

"So what has Betty gotten herself into this time?" Betty was his latest cartoon character. She'd shown up over a year ago in a drawing and had been a constant in his work since then. Betty coincidentally bore a striking resemblance to...well, Bridget.

"Her boss has asked her for a favor and now she finds herself in a bit of trouble."

"I don't know where you get your ideas," Bridget said sarcastically.

He smiled innocently. "They just come to me. Hey, can I use that shoe bit?"

"Sure. Mock my life. As long as it brings a chuckle to you, that's all that matters."

"Speaking of mocking, your mother called," Richard told her, pulling his drawings back to his side of the desk. "She wants to know why you were on television trying to get a husband when you have such a wonderful man like me in your life."

"Did you explain how you sold me into the servitude of Breathe Better Mouthwash?"

"I told her it was my fault. I begged her for forgiveness.

She asked me if I was coming for Christmas, to which I said yes. There, you see? I'm not all bad."

"Not *all* bad."

Richard glanced again at the now mysterious dress. "So you're all set for next week?"

"Hardly. I've got a facial, a pedicure and a manicure all scheduled for this weekend. This whole caving into society and trying to live up to impossible physical standards is exhausting work. I don't know how women do it on a regular basis."

"Practice," Richard guessed. "Were you planning on spending any time here at the office?"

She shook her head. "After all that is done, Raquel is going to try and fit me in with Lars—"

"Lars?"

"Her hairstyling boyfriend."

"You mean ex-boyfriend."

"Right," Bridget affirmed even as she was rolling her eyes. "She wants to get me in with him the day of the show to do my do."

"Mountain Dew?"

"Hairdo," she corrected, although she knew he knew what she meant. He was just being difficult. She was curious as to why. After all, putting her on the show had been his idea. Granted, he hadn't expected her to make the first cut, but now that she had, he seemed almost surly about it and she didn't think it was just about her missing work. "Anyway, then Raquel will do my makeup right before we go live."

Richard scowled a little. "That's an awful lot of effort for a guy you don't even like."

"How do I know if I don't like him?" Bridget pointed out. "I haven't really gotten to know him."

"Trust me. With Brock, what you see is what you get. The man is as fake as his capped teeth and sunless tan."

"That's unfair. He might have hidden depths to him. Levels to his character that even he isn't aware of. He is an actor. Surely he has to pull from some internal emotional wellspring. If not, then maybe I will bring something out in him that no other woman has."

Richard's scowl increased tenfold. "You're not serious. You're not actually interested in a soap opera actor?"

Hmm, Bridget mused. Was that jealousy she heard in the subtle undertones of his shouting?

"Like I said, I don't know him well enough to know whether I like him or not. But he certainly deserves a chance. Let's put aside the fact that he picked me over several other beautiful women—"

"You know," he stated, cutting her off, very obviously irritated. "You're not dog meat. Or horrifically disfigured in some way. It's not the biggest shock in the world that you were selected."

"You said before the show even began that there was no way he was going to pick me. Until the end you had me pegged as one of the losers."

"Because of the sort of person he is and the type of woman I imagined he might be attracted to, not because of you," Richard clarified. "You're not ugly."

"Thank you," she beamed, tucking that little gem of a compliment away to savor the next time he ticked her off for some reason. "But let's put that aside for now. The truth is I'm not getting any younger."

"You're twenty-eight!" He said that as if it were the youngest age on the planet.

"I agree. It's not ancient. I just think it's time I got a real boyfriend. Not just a pretend one. As wonderful as you are in the role, there is a little something...missing."

Judging by his facial expression, this clearly incensed him and Bridget had to stifle her laughter in the face of his blossoming outrage. She found herself wondering at the cause of it. In the past few minutes, he'd expressed jealousy over Brock, told her she wasn't ugly and now he was getting angry at the idea of being dumped, when he wasn't even her real boyfriend in the first place.

Was it possible that the wedding had changed something for him, too?

She tried to remember if his behavior had been different since then, but there was nothing she could put her finger on. Sure, he had asked her to hang around the office more than ever, but that could be blamed on the demands of the Breathe Better campaign. A few times he'd offered to walk her to the subway, but that could be construed as protecting his interests—if she ever got mugged and was laid up in a hospital, he'd never find any of his folders.

Still, she had a feeling. A sort of awareness. Sometimes she'd look up from her stool to find him staring at her, but whenever she asked him about it, he would brush her off and tell her he was just thinking. Yet last night he'd told her she was the woman he would have picked. Now he was furious. So what did it all mean? Bridget didn't know, but that didn't mean she couldn't have some fun with him.

"What do you mean something missing? Am I not attentive?" Richard demanded.

"You are."

"Am I not the picture of a respectable boyfriend?"

"You are."

"So what's the problem?" he practically shouted.

"It's just that I'm looking for...what's the word...? Action."

"Action!"

"You know kissing, hand holding, hugging. Sex."

His face was nearly purple by this point, which actually brought out the green in his hazel eyes. "You're saying you want to have sex with Brock?"

"I'm saying that I want to have sex with someone," Bridget corrected him, playing this out for all she was worth. "Brock just happens to be available. He finds me attractive, and let's face it, he didn't get the title of heartthrob for nothing."

Instinctively, Richard straightened to his full six-foot-three-inch height. "You think he's handsome?"

"Blond hair. Blue eyes. Buff. Who wouldn't?"

"It's just that I never pegged you as falling for that obvious sort of attractiveness. I assumed you would look deeper into a man's mind. His heart."

"The brain and the heart are both well and good," Bridget agreed. "But when it comes to sex, it doesn't hurt to have a hottie in the sack."

Richard huffed and focused his attention back on his boxes of drawings. Bridget watched him and waited.

One minute later he lifted his head. "Are you trying to say that I'm not handsome enough to be your fake boyfriend?"

"Absolutely not," she stated truthfully. Since the first day she'd come to work for him, she'd known he was handsome. Then he'd yelled at her for moving his pencils, which caused his overall attractiveness to diminish significantly. It was only recently that she found herself assessing his physical attributes once again. He was most definitely two thumbs up.

"I'm tall," Richard stated. "Sure, more lean than buff, but that's just because I'm too busy seeing to our future to get to the gym as often as I would like. But I'm no weakling."

"You do have trouble opening pickle jars," she pointed out.

"For Pete's sake! No one can open those on the first try."

"True," she allowed.

"So I don't have blond hair."

"I like sandy brown," she said quietly. Actually, his color

hair was her favorite because it changed with the seasons, getting lighter in summer and darker in winter. Each season provided a whole new reason to be attracted to him.

"And sure he has blue eyes, but are they real?" Richard wanted to know.

"Hazel can be a very compelling color."

"Thank you!" he shouted as if winning some kind of moral victory.

"Okay."

Richard eyed her suspiciously now. He couldn't say why, but he felt as if he had fallen into some carefully laid trap. "Okay, what?"

"Okay, you can have sex with me if you want," she blurted out.

"What!"

"You're standing there telling me how handsome you are and how you are so much better for me than Brock, I just assumed you were trying to proposition me."

And if he was trying to proposition her, then she had just said yes. Oh, yeah, things definitely were getting weird between them.

"Don't be ridiculous." He struggled a little to find his breath and as a result didn't quite catch the fleeting look of disappointment that crossed her face. He had to wait until his heart stopped beating quite so hard before he could speak again. "You work for me."

"Right. Ridiculous. What was I thinking?" she said, exhaling slowly. "Look, my ankle really hurts. Do you mind if I go home early? It looks like you've got everything under control for the new client coming in later this afternoon."

Richard followed her gaze to the folder on the credenza behind him and the preliminary storyboards he had drawn up.

"I do."

"Remember, they are going to want to buy ad time on TV. Tell them they can reach the teen market just as effectively and for significantly less money with print ads in magazines."

"I got all your research and notes," he told her. "And it's just an introduction."

"You're sure you don't need me? I could stay. It's just that Raquel outlined this whole body beauty treatment for me that I'd better start working on if I want to fit in all the stages by next week."

"Go. I've got everything ready." And thanks to that whole sex conversation, he very much needed time to gather his wits. Wits that had been blown to the four corners of the universe with her shocking announcement that he could have sex with her. "Do you need help?"

"I can make it. See you tomorrow." Gently, she lowered herself off the stool and limped back to the coat rack to retrieve her dress. He watched as she steadily made her way down the hall until she finally reached the elevator at the far end of the building.

As soon as the doors closed behind her, he slumped down onto the stool behind him that he very rarely used.

Sex? With Bridget? It was untenable. She was his assistant. He was her boss. Basically she was going to be his partner in his new agency. She had one of the finest analytical marketing brains in the country as far as he was concerned and would be the key to making his business a great success. Then there was the way they worked together—like a choreographed dance, it seemed so effortless at times.

She was able to predict his needs, accommodate his moods and make him laugh whenever he started to take himself too seriously. Not to mention she provided stellar material for his comic-strip character, Betty. But that was it.

They were colleagues. Friends. Partners. A team. Not lovers.

Unfortunately, he had a suspicion where her sudden craving for sex was coming from. It was possible that he'd laid it on a little too thick when he'd taken her to her sister's wedding. It's just that he knew what it was like not to measure up to a parent's expectations or a sibling's accomplishments. He knew all too well. And he didn't want that for her.

It had been a fun night. They'd danced and cavorted, playing the part of lovers to the hilt. The whole time laughing at how easily they were fooling everyone.

It had been easy. Easy to hold her close while they danced because, despite their height differential, they seemed to fit together pretty well. He'd had no problem whispering in her ear because she'd used a special flower shampoo that had smelled really nice. Gazing into her eyes had been a little bit of a hassle, but that was just because of the damn glasses she insisted on wearing.

Still, he hadn't meant to suggest anything with all of his flirting. She hadn't gone and done something incredibly stupid like fall for him, had she?

Nah. It wasn't possible. Nothing had changed in the months since the wedding. They were business as usual. Maybe they were working a little longer these days, lingering over working dinners, staying later on the weekends together, but that was just because of the show. No way had she developed a crush on him. She just had been baiting him with all that talk of sex.

That's all it was. They didn't think of each other like that.

Okay. It *was* possible that he had thought about her like that from time to time. A brief, harmless thought that came and went faster than a sneeze. But that was just because he was a man. All men thought about what it would be like to have sex with the women in their lives even if they weren't necessarily physically attracted to them.

Okay, okay. Maybe he was a little attracted to her, he admitted to himself. However, it certainly wasn't a full-fledged attraction. Merely a flicker. A hint of something that had sparked to life between them the first time he'd danced with her. But that didn't mean he would act on it. There were rules about this sort of thing and the biggest, most important rule of all was never to get involved with the assistant. Things invariably ended badly and then he would be stuck with a temp.

Nothing was worse then a temp.

Richard shook off all thoughts of any kind of romantic liaison between him and Bridget. In fact, he wanted to dismiss her from his thoughts altogether. He'd spent way too much time thinking about her as it was. He needed to focus. He only had about an hour left before the new client came in to meet with him, and he wanted to finish this sequence of boxes.

He stared down at the face in his drawings and realized that putting Bridget out of his mind was going to be a lot easier said then done.

"HURRY, LARS. The show goes on in an hour and I still have to do her makeup," Raquel insisted.

"Ah cannot be rushed," Lars protested in an accent that Bridget hadn't quite yet identified. "Ah am an artist."

Oh, please, Bridget thought. *Spare me from any more artists.* She'd been primped, buffed, polished and waxed by artists in the last few days. Lars was just the most recent. He'd been unable to work her into his fantastically busy schedule at the salon, but as a favor to his ex-girlfriend, he'd come to the Long Island house with his supplies to do Bridget's hair before the show. They were in one of the bedrooms upstairs where Bridget was made to sit still, knees uncrossed, in his special foldaway chair. Meanwhile Raquel hovered and Lars cut.

And cut. And cut.

"You're sure you're not taking off too much. You know I typically like to wear my hair back in a bun or a ponytail during the day."

"Yes, ah know. Theese is ridiculous."

Bridget didn't know why she bothered. It's not as if she'd had any say since this beauty journey began. Raquel picked her nail color and her eyebrow design, which Bridget was stunned to find out wasn't some kind of joke. Then there was the mandatory bikini wax.

Pain took on a whole new level at that point.

Fortunately, the pedicure came soon after, and that was a delightful experience. The truth was, and Bridget was almost loath to admit this to herself, it had been sort of fun— except for the bikini wax. Her skin was smooth, her eyes had a new definition and her toes and fingernails sparkled. She felt pampered from head to toe, inside and out. And although she might be giving Lars a hard time, she was actually anticipating the new cut.

A clump of hair dropped in front of her eyes, and she gulped. Okay, maybe *anticipating* was the wrong word.

"And I don't want bangs. I said that, right? No bangs. Under any circumstances." Another clump of hair fell in front of her face.

"Yes, ah know. Theese is ridiculous, too."

Everything was ridiculous to Lars. Bridget decided that, although the name was Swedish, the accent was definitely something close to French.

"Tell me, Lars. Where are you from originally?"

"Paramus, New Jersey."

Well, then, that explained the accent.

"Lars started speaking with a Swedish accent to go with his name. He thought it would help business," Raquel explained.

"But he sounds French."

"Ah du?"

Snip. There went another chunk of hair. It didn't matter. In fact, she had always considered the Sinead O'Connor look very sexy.

"Lars, honey, please hurry."

"Eh, eh, eh. Ex-honey."

"Oh, that's right," Raquel gasped. "Ex-sweetie, will you please hurry?"

"Ex-darling, ah told you, ah cannot be rushed."

"But ex-lover, I haven't even started on her foundation."

"Yes, but ex-sugar puff—"

"Oh, all right already," Bridget exclaimed. "Guys, I know you two are still together."

Raquel looked at Lars apologetically and shrugged. "She's very clever."

"My Raquel wants to be an actress. Ah want this for her."

"Okay, but you do realize that if she wins, she's going to have to marry Brock."

"No! This ah cannot allow. Ah will kill him first," Lars said passionately.

"Could you make sure you do that off camera? Blood isn't really good for ratings," Bridget quipped, assuming that Lars had been joking.

But when he nodded firmly and said, "Ah will try," she got a little nervous.

"Now please, everyone, ah must have quiet. It is time for the next phase."

That sounded ominous.

"Blow-drying," Raquel announced in a breathy tone that spoke of reverence.

When blow-drying was finished, there was styling. After styling, there was setting. After setting, there was primping. After primping, there was studying. After studying, Lars backed away from her chair and shouted, "Finis!"

Raquel giggled and whispered to Bridget, "He makes me so hot when he speaks Swedish."

Bridget didn't argue. "Can I see a mirror?" She was very curious whether or not she actually had any hair left because most of it seemed to be piled on the plastic mat that Lars had placed under her chair.

"Mirror later. Makeup next," Raquel told her as she began to apply foundation. "You'll see. When I get done with you, Richard won't know what hit him."

"Richard? You mean Brock. I'm here to seduce Brock."

Raquel looked confused. Then she said "Ohh," as a light apparently dawned. "I get it. You want to seduce Brock to make Richard jealous. Very tricky."

Bridget gulped. "Jealous? No. Why...why...would you say that? I don't...do not...at all...want to make Richard jealous," she stuttered somewhat hysterically. "That's silly. He's my boss. I'm his assistant."

"Look up," Raquel instructed, as she carefully combed Bridget's bottom eyelashes with the mascara. "Yes, but you do have feelings for him."

"That is the most ridiculous... Why? Why? Why do you think that?"

"It was obvious at the ice-cream place. First, you stole his cherry and then you offered him the rest of your sundae. Only a woman in love wouldn't be able to eat a whole sundae. But since you two aren't a couple yet, I had to guess that you were trying to use this show to make him jealous."

It was true, Bridget thought. She had stolen his cherry. And handing over the sundae was her equivalent of flirting.

Richard had finished the ice cream, smothered a burp and clapped her on the back in thanks. So, all things considered, it wasn't necessarily a success. And of course, there was the incident last week in his office when he'd told her not to be "ridiculous." That had hurt. It was true that she hadn't had a whole lot of lovers in her life, but no one had ever said that sleeping with her would be ridiculous.

"Ooh is this Richard?" Lars wanted to know.

"He's my boss. That's all," Bridget insisted, even though she knew—really had known for some time—that it was a lie. "Besides, he's impossible to deal with. He's moody and arrogant. And he's always picking on me. "

They both stared at her.

"Okay," she allowed. "It's possible that I might have begun to feel...something. Something very vague and completely insubstantial. I'm sure it's a passing illness. It will go away."

Still they stared.

"Sure, we're friends. Not even friends really. More like...friendly. We're friendly colleagues who... Oh, forget it!" she cried even as she began to hyperventilate. "Fine, I confess. It's true. I didn't want to believe it. I've been trying to fight it. But I don't think I can anymore. I've done the stupidest, most completely idiotic thing ever imaginable...I've fallen for my boss."

"You should never fall for your boss. Theese is ridiculous."

"Thanks for the advice," Bridget growled.

"But if it is too late, then there is nothing you can do."

Oh, there was something she could do. She could get over him. She could tell Raquel to stop with the war paint and stop trying to be someone she was not. And she could stop using this stupid show as a way to make Richard notice her, which, now that she was being completely honest with herself, was the only reason she had agreed to go on in the first place.

"Ah have a suggestion."

Or she could listen to Lars. After all, he was an artist and French.

"You should make this Richard jealous by seducing Brock."

"Uh, hello?" Bridget retorted. "Dress, hair, shoes, makeup. That plan is already in play. But it's never going to work. I can't seduce anyone. Let alone a heartthrob!" Bridget wailed.

"Oh, no, no crying. You'll cause creases in my makeup." That said, Raquel went back to powdering and brushing.

"To seduce a man you must be alluring," Lars instructed her. "You must be a temptress. You must look at Brock like he is your sun and your moon."

"Or maybe I could just be myself."

Lars looked at Raquel, who shrugged her shoulders and shook her head slightly as if to suggest there was only so much they could do.

Lars sighed. "It is a good thing that you have excellent hair."

RICHARD PACED the foyer of the mansion and checked his watch for the fifth time.

"Yo, chicks! Places!" Buzz shouted, sending the six women in the room scrambling for their seats amongst the white couches and love seats. Buzz surveyed the room and frowned. "Richard. I've only got six. I'm supposed to have eight. You know what it means when I have six and I'm supposed to have eight?"

"The shot is going to be uneven?"

"The shot is going to be uneven," he repeated.

"She's coming," Raquel announced. "Oh, and I'm coming, too." Raquel descended the wide curving stairs that led to the foyer taking each step as if the cameras were already on her. She smiled and even waved a little. As soon as she reached the bottom, she sashayed to the living room and filled one of the empty spaces.

All eyes were now pinned to the top of the stairs. Richard heard the gasps of the other girls, but was too occupied with the scene there to really notice the sound.

Someone was standing on the upper landing. Someone who was not his Bridget. Or was it? The height was about right. Perhaps a little taller than usual. The figure was hers, although it was shown off to spectacular perfection in a red dress that clung to her body in all the right places. Her shoulders looked creamy. And the dip in front of the dress hinted at actual cleavage. Loose wisps of dark hair flirted around her impossibly big eyes and fell in soft waves over her shoulders. She wasn't the most spectacularly beautiful woman on the planet, but boy, she sure was pretty.

"Bridget?"

She smiled and started to make her way down the stairs, instantly tripping in her high-heeled shoes. She grabbed for the railing and tried to hold herself up, but her momentum carried her down a few more steps before she was able to right herself.

Yep, that was his Bridget.

After Bridget steadied herself, she flipped back her hair, straightened her skirt and placed a hand on one hip in a gesture that Raquel had assured her was seductive.

"Richard," she said coolly as soon as she reached the bottom steps. She didn't stop, but moved past him carelessly on her way to the living room where the crew, the women and Brock were waiting.

"Bridget!"

"What?" she asked turning around and losing her balance in the process.

Richard reached out and grabbed her arm to steady her, his face pressed up against hers. "Where the hell is the rest of that dress?"

She craned her neck as if to peer over her shoulder at the skin she must have known was visible. "You mean this dress?"

"Bridget," he growled in a way that let her know he was serious. "You can't wear that dress on TV."

"Why not? It's no skimpier than their dresses," she said pointing to the women already in place.

"Because...because..."

She tilted her head. "This is the point where you should realize you have absolutely no reason for saying what you are saying."

"Your mother is going to be watching."

He could see her eye twitch slightly. "I can live with that. Now, if you'll excuse me, I believe we're ready to go live."

"In ten, nine, eight..." Buzz counted down.

Bridget scurried as quickly as her shoes would allow and found the last empty spot on the couch. She beamed into the camera, her satisfaction at Richard's obvious agitation written all over her face.

Chuck stood in the center of the room, his back to most of the women. As soon as he saw Buzz's fist close, he broke into his speech.

"Good evening, ladies and gentlemen and welcome back to *Who Wants To Marry a Heartthrob?*"

Bridget barely listened to the introduction. She was still coming to grips with the fact that she had finally admitted, out loud, what had been simmering inside her for some time. She had feelings for Richard. There was no denying it now. And since she'd gone so far as to get herself on television, she figured she might as well take it all the way.

Her goal: to grab a few moments alone with Brock so she could secure her selection for next week's show. Richard definitely was agitated by her new look, her dress, all of it. If it was the show that was making that reaction happen, then her choice was to continue with it.

Or she could sit down with Richard and have a serious and mature discussion about her feelings.

Cornering Brock it was.

Chuck gave the go-ahead for the intimate cocktail party to begin and Brock worked the room like a seasoned pro, stopping to chat with each woman—some in groups, others one-on-one. He smiled. He flirted. He made every woman in the room feel like a queen.

Bridget needed to talk to him, but she didn't want to do that on camera. She waited for the first commercial, then as casually as she could on three-inch heels, she wandered over to the French doors that overlooked the backyard. In the distance, the moonlight gleamed off the water of the inlet. The patio was set with subtle lanterns that illuminated the space, but still gave the impression of intimacy.

With what she hoped was a come-hither look, Bridget caught Brock's attention before she opened the doors and wandered outside. It was a massive area designed for entertaining, complete with a grill, a table and several chairs. But as soon as Bridget stepped out, she realized she had made a critical mistake.

It was freezing and she was wearing nothing more than panties and a flimsy dress. She'd forgone a wrap because she hadn't wanted to cover the back of her dress and stockings because Raquel had said that stockings were out. Bridget had no idea when that happened, but as her legs turned to goose pimples and her arms collapsed in on herself in an effort to keep warm, she decided she was going to lodge a formal complaint with the fashion police and demand that stockings be let back in.

"Hi. You're Bridget."

"Y-y-y...y-yes-s..." she said as she tried to gain control over her teeth.

"Cold, huh." Brock took off his jacket and wrapped it around her shoulders. Immediately, the warmth of the coat alleviated the worst of her chills and she was able to speak again.

"Thank you."

"Sure. I'm glad you came out here. I sort of wanted a chance to talk to you privately. That's really hard to do inside with all the cameras around. They're everywhere."

"Comes with the fact that it's a reality TV show I guess."

"Oh, yeah. Anyway, after the commercial they're going to do some one-on-one interviews with the women inside, so we have a few minutes."

"Perfect," she purred. Or at least she hoped it was a purr. It might have been more of a growl.

"So, here's the thing, I'm going to pick you in the next round, okay?"

Bridget beamed. This was much easier than she'd thought it would be. Or maybe she was more seductive than she gave herself credit for. Apparently, Brock couldn't resist her. Then she felt somewhat guilty. What if he really liked her? It wouldn't be fair to lead him on, not after she'd finally admitted to herself what she felt for Richard.

"That's great, Brock. But I think I should tell you, as flattered as I am to be chosen, there is someone else..."

"Oh, no, it's not like that. I'm not hot for you or anything."

"Excellent," she hissed, feeling the air being let out of her ego. "Then why me?"

"Because you don't hassle me like the other women do." Brock sat on one of the patio chairs. "They're always pulling on me and trying to get me to kiss them."

Bridget walked over and sat on one of the chairs across from him, careful not to let her bare legs touch the cold wrought iron. "I'm confused. You're a guy and you've got all these beautiful women trying to kiss you. Isn't that supposed to be like guy heaven?"

"Sure, I guess," Brock mumbled. "For some guys."

Bridget stared at him, hard. He glanced up at her shyly and the answer was written all over his face. "Brock, are you trying to tell me...?"

"I'm gay."

4

"YOU'RE gay!"

"Shh. Shh," Brock hushed her. "Not so loud. Do you want everyone to hear?"

Bridget considered this. "Uh, yes. I think so. I think all of those women in there who are competing to be your wife should know that you are, in fact...gay!"

His face tightened. "I see. You're one of those people who have a problem with men who live an alternate lifestyle."

Bridget bristled at the accusation. "I have no problem with men who want to live an alternate lifestyle, Brock. I do, however, have a big problem with someone who wants to do that and be married to a woman!"

He shrugged off her concern. "It's not like this thing is really going to end in a marriage. It's just a TV show."

"A *reality* TV show," Bridget reminded him. "Emphasis on the word *reality*. Those women in there think that one of them is going to marry you and live happily ever after."

This time he actually snorted. "Those women in there think they are going to be famous. They don't care about me."

"Fine," Bridget relented, not doubting the truth of that statement after her conversations with Raquel. "But why go out of your way to be on a show where you're bound to get hassled by lots of women?"

"I need this," he insisted. His urgency was evident in the tone of his voice and the intensity in his baby-blue eyes.

Bridget could tell this was no act. Brock simply didn't have that much talent as an actor.

"I've been off my soap for almost a month now. A few more weeks and I'll be totally forgotten!"

"Why did they fire you?"

"I was always doing love scenes! Love scenes and more love scenes. I spent all of last year practically naked. I wanted a serious storyline. Something like a heroin addiction or possibly even making me a closet kleptomaniac."

"Oh, sure, kleptomania, that's serious."

"Anyway, one of the producers didn't like my attitude and told me to take a hike. At first I thought I would be picked up by another soap, but everyone knows me as Dr. Noah Vanderhorn. I'm stuck with it. Which means I need to get that part back."

"What about something else? Maybe commercials," she suggested.

"I can't. I'm too good-looking for most commercials," he lamented. "They want, you know, ordinary people for that. I'm special."

Bridget rolled her eyes. "Well, it's good to know that after a month away from TV, your ego's still intact."

"I know," he replied in relief, clearly not understanding that Bridget hadn't been offering a compliment. "But that's the only thing I've kept. My life has no meaning anymore. At least when I was on the show I used to be someone. I was a doctor. A surgeon."

"You were an actor!" And evidently a delusional one at that, she thought.

"But I *played* a doctor. I could say things like 'ccs' and 're-suscitate.' I saved lives. In the operating room I was an artist."

Another artist! Exactly when did people learn how to

become these so-called artists? Bridget wondered. And why wasn't anyone simply good at his or her job anymore?

"I have to get back on *Many Days*. I know that as soon as the producers see me again, they'll know they made a mistake and ask me back."

Focusing once again on the gay, delusional soap star, Bridget shook her head. "Look Brock, I'm not sure what you want me to do. I have to tell Richard about this."

"You can't. He might cancel everything."

"With good reason. The Breathe Better Mouthwash people are paying big money for this show to promote their product. I think they might be slightly alarmed that their heartthrob in question is secretly attracted to the host instead of the contestants."

"Chuck and I are just friends," Brock said. Nowhere near as convincingly as she said it when she was referring to her and Richard.

"Unbelievable," she muttered, trying not to think about what went on back in the *contemplation area*.

"If the Breathe Better Mouthwash people walk, then the show gets canceled. Right? That means your boss would lose the client, the money, everything."

Bridget bit her bottom lip. Brock was right. If the show failed—and cancellation was pretty much the biggest failure she could imagine—there was a very good chance that Richard would lose the account. In addition to that, if the show was canceled, V.I.P. would be on the hook for all the production expenses. Not only would Richard not get his opportunity to leave the agency, he might lose his job over this account.

Where Richard went, she was sure to follow. Even if that meant right out onto the street.

But her job was the least of her concerns. It was Richard's reaction that worried her. She knew what this show meant to him. He'd put too much time and effort into making it a success for it to fail now. Not to mention, he was convinced that his future was riding on it. Their future. How could she tell him the truth about Brock and jeopardize all of that?

Especially when she was the one who was responsible for doing all the background checks on the contestants. It never had occurred to her that she needed to check out Brock, too. *Fool*, she reprimanded herself. Why didn't she think to ask Brock if he was gay? How silly of her to assume that a man who volunteered to go on a dating show where all the contestants were women would be straight.

Bridget covered her face with her hands, then quickly removed them for fear of smudging her makeup. Mascara could be a bitch when it smudged.

One thing was for sure, the timing of all of this was a disaster. Here she was just coming to grips with her feelings for Richard, only to turn around and possibly sink his career. A career that he had invested all of himself in. Getting him fired definitely would not be a great way to start a romance. If all she had to do was keep a secret for a few weeks, then so be it. It was the least she could do for him.

And of course, if by staying on the show—which she was now guaranteed—she was able to provoke Richard's jealousy to such a level that he actually would begin to notice her as a woman and not just as an assistant... Well, that was just gravy.

Brock must have sensed her weakening. "Come on," he coaxed. "What's the big deal if you don't say anything? The show goes on, the mouthwash people get what they want, Richard gets what he wants and I'll keep picking you to fend off the others."

"Fend them off? Have you met Jenna?"

"Yeah, she's pretty tough. But I have to keep picking her, too."

"Why?"

"Do you see how good we look together? We're a casting director's dream team. Only she keeps blocking my light."

"And I don't."

"Right," Brock exclaimed. "You don't hassle me and you don't upstage me. You're perfect."

For some reason Bridget didn't feel flattered by Brock's idea of perfection. "Okay. For argument's sake, let's say I keep my mouth shut and play the role of blocker for you. What exactly does that mean?"

"It means I'll keep picking you until the final round. I figured you're only here to make Richard jealous anyway and me giving you the green card should do the trick."

Immediately, Bridget flushed red. Had she been that obvious? "I'm only doing this because Bambi got her boobs too big."

Brock tilted his head and shot her a knowing glance. Bridget's shoulders slumped. She was not a great liar. "How can you tell?"

"It's the way you look at him," he said.

She should consider carrying around a video camera and taping herself so she could see what everyone else obviously saw. "Fine. You win. I stay until the last round. But so help me, you say one word to Richard about my feelings and I confess the whole thing."

"Deal."

"And you have to treat me like all the other girls," Bridget added. "I want to be romanced and told my eyes are big and my skin is soft."

"No problem. Seducing women is my bread and butter," Brock told her. "In front of a camera that is."

"You really think all of this is worth it just to get back on a soap opera?" she had to ask.

"Not *a* soap opera. *The* soap opera. *The Many Days of Life* is no joke. They address the serious issues facing today's culture."

Bridget's lips twitched. "You got that from *TV Guide*, didn't you?"

He smiled in return. It was a beautiful smile. "Yeah. But how cool does that sound? I've got to get back. I just have to."

"Is that physically possible for your character? How were you...terminated?"

Brock's eyes lit up. "Oh, it's cool. They sent me to Mexico to learn experimental holistic treatments. Originally, I was supposed to be eaten by a shark while swimming in the waters off the coast of Mexico, but an old boyfriend is one of the writers and he did me a favor and kept them from having me eaten."

"What a break."

"You're telling me," Brock agreed. "Now, do we have a deal?"

He offered his hand and Bridget couldn't help the sinking feeling that she was making a deal with the devil. But if it was the devil she needed to negotiate with to win Richard's heart, she'd do it. "Deal."

Brock stood up then and she stood, too, not realizing how close together they were. For a second she lost her balance and he had to reach out to steady her. Neither one of them noticed the cameraman standing just inside the French doors.

RICHARD STOOD in the foyer of the house. Removed from the temporary set of the living room, he watched cameramen circle the white space filming different pairings of women, no doubt hoping to catch two of them in a spontaneous cat fight. Dan and Don—it was easier when they were together because he didn't have to remember who was who—stood behind him, their eyes glued to the small TV monitor that was relaying the live broadcast.

Every few minutes Richard turned around to take in their expressions. He concluded they must like what they were seeing because the two of them were riveted to the television. He stopped himself from rubbing his hands together in jubilation and considered what he'd accomplished with this show.

One small step for singledom; one giant leap for mouthwash.

Richard chuckled inwardly at his own joke and then considered writing the line down for use on a future commercial.

Maybe a shot on the moon. Bad breath fogging up a space helmet. Then a shot of Breathe Better Mouthwash and bang—the glass in front of the helmet is clear and the astronaut is smiling because he doesn't have to smell his own halitosis anymore. There would have to be a woman there. Maybe an alien?

Instantly, Richard slapped a hand over his eyes to stop the horrific images in his head. He must be more bothered by Bridget's appearance than he thought to allow himself even to consider such a ridiculous idea.

It was the red dress, he decided. It haunted him. Or rather, the lack of it did. What was she thinking prancing around in such an outfit?

Of course he knew what she was thinking. She wanted to look nice for TV. No, not nice. Naughty. She wanted to look seductive like the other women did. She wanted to compete with them on their turf. Only that was impossible.

Bridget wasn't that kind of girl. She was simple and plain. And he liked her that way.

There wasn't a whole lot of fuss about Bridget. She

didn't complain if she got caught in the rain and her clothes were ruined. She didn't whine on windy days when wisps of hair escaped her bun. She didn't need to replace her lipstick every five minutes. She didn't make him wait for hours on those evenings when he dragged her out to a client's wrap-up party.

That's why he was so bothered by her new appearance, he decided. He didn't like to see anyone doing something that was so intrinsically against character, and everything about this show was anti-Bridget. He was sure it would be just a matter of time before she realized that and stopped going to such lengths to impress Brock.

Or more likely, all of this would end when she didn't make it to the next round. Sure, she looked great in the dress tonight, but he was still counting on Brock's shallowness to pick the flashier contestants to continue. Among the eight women in this group, the new Bridget still ranked as the least flashy.

Satisfied with his conclusions, Richard glanced down at his watch. Only another few minutes to go until the invitation ceremony where she would pick up her red card and return to being the unassuming assistant he knew her to be.

"Hey, look at that," Dan or Don said. "Who would have thought he'd go for the shy one?"

"I know. But did you see her back in that dress? Yum."

Richard turned at the sound of Dan or Don's comments. Shy one? Back? Yum? "What's going on?"

The executive pointed to the monitor. "The camera guy caught Brock and the quiet girl out on the patio together. I think he's about to kiss her."

"What? Oh, for Pete's sake will you two stop ogling her!" Richard shoved the two men out of the way and stared at the monitor. There she was. His Bridget wearing

Brock's coat. His hands were on her arms and he was bending down toward her almost as if he was going to...

Just then the French doors flew open, and Jenna in all her dramatic glory stepped out onto the patio. "What do you think you're doing?"

"Uh, Jenna. Hi. We were just talking," Brock told the brunette, even as he took a step back from Bridget.

With the sudden release of his hands from around her upper arms, Bridget faltered a little bit. The fact that she wasn't exactly a pro on the heels yet didn't help, either. After stumbling back a few steps she was finally able to regain her balance. A good thing, too, because Jenna was immediately in her face.

"What do you think you're doing?"

Bridget considered the question but wasn't really sure what the appropriate answer was. Admitting that she was making a deal with Brock to hide his secret and protect Richard's show, while at the same time making Richard so insanely jealous he would recognize his subconscious feelings for her, didn't exactly feel right.

"We were talking." She figured she would start with that.

"Sure you were." Jenna's reply was thick with sarcasm. "Then why are you wearing his coat?"

"I was cold."

"Do you honestly expect us to believe that?"

Bridget didn't really think it was a matter of belief so much as it was a fact. However, before she could answer she realized the other women had gathered around them along with all of the cameramen. All eyes were pinned on her, and she found herself thrust into a position she traditionally loathed: the spotlight.

She'd spent a lifetime avoiding this very thing at family weddings, school dances, office parties, and now here she was in the center of all these people. To top it all off, she was doing it on television. She tried not to scrunch up her face in misery and figured the quickest way out of this mess was to let Jenna play out her lines. On the plus side, watching an actress like Jenna in action could be a learning experience. Part of Bridget was sorry she didn't have a pen and paper to take notes.

The taller woman flipped her long, dark hair over one shoulder and crossed her arms under her breasts. "You think you're so smart, but I'm on to your act."

"You are?" Bridget winced, wondering if Jenna was about to announce to the television audience that Bridget was only on the show to make Richard jealous. Everyone else had picked up on it, so it wouldn't have surprised her if Jenna knew, too.

"You've got the role of the shy, quiet, mousy girl down pat," Jenna accused her. "But you can't fool me. You lured Brock out here away from the rest of us. Then you got him to take off his coat. What was next? His pants?"

Bridget wanted to laugh at the idea, but the cameras were moving in closer and the red lights above them were shining in her eyes, causing her to blink.

"No. We were... We were just talking," Bridget tried again. She looked to Brock for help. But he was playing along with the scene that Jenna had created and was now looking at Bridget suspiciously, as though he was wondering if she had tricked him into venturing onto the patio.

The cameras turned back to Jenna, and Bridget conceded that the woman was a natural. Her eyes were damp with tears. Her lips were trembling. Hell, even Bridget was buying the act. Maybe after the show, she could get Jenna to show her how she made her bottom lip puffy like that.

"I came here looking for love. I wanted to find a soul mate. And I think I might have found him in Brock. But every time I want to talk to him, you're there. Pulling him away. Not just from me. From all of us. We all have a right to get to know Brock, too. That's all we want, Bridget. Won't you please just let us do that?"

Before Bridget could answer, Chuck walked out on to the patio. "I'm sorry ladies, but our time is up. The party is over."

"Oh, thank you, God," Bridget whispered to no one in particular.

"If you'll all retire to the living room, I'll escort Brock off to make his very difficult decision." One of the cameramen swung his camera toward Chuck who smiled brilliantly, his teeth practically glowing in the darkness of evening. "We'll be right back after these commercials brought to you, as always, by Breathe Better Mouthwash, the mouthwash choice of singles. Because your *future* may depend on it."

The cameras blinked off and Bridget stumbled back to the patio chair she'd been sitting on before, desperately thankful that she'd managed that scene without doing anything too embarrassing. Both Chuck and Brock were gone. And the three cameramen, led by Buzz, went back inside to set up for the last group shot of the night.

Only the women remained. When Bridget glanced up she could see that all of them were still glaring at her, except for Raquel, who was checking her hair in the reflection of the glass doors.

"I don't think we should do patio scenes anymore. This damp air is not good for the state of my curls," she announced.

As soon as the words were out of her mouth the other women immediately ran in search of the nearest reflective surface to determine for themselves if their appearance had been compromised by the impromptu visit outside. Jenna, however, stood like an Amazon in front of the doors.

"Hey, great scene," Bridget complimented her as she made her way toward the doors. "That whole bit about the soul mate, did you make that up on the fly?"

"It's a gift," Jenna said smugly.

"See, I figured you for the villainous bitch, but I guess this means you're auditioning for the role of the hapless female ingénue," Bridget surmised.

Jenna moved her neck in such a way as to send her hair swooshing perfectly over her right shoulder. Even before Lars had hacked off half her hair, Bridget would never have been able to do that. It was really quite an impressive trick.

"It's not like I didn't consider the role of the villainous bitch," Jenna explained. "But let's face it. A daytime soap typically only has one of those per show. Much more opportunity this way."

"I don't know. You would have made a really good bitch."

Jenna's smile only widened. "Just stay out of my way, Minnie Mouse."

With that she turned, and Bridget watched in amazement as once again her hair moved in coordination with the rest of her body, rearranging itself perfectly down her back. Bridget wondered if Jenna had to send her hair to obedience school for a few months to get it to do that.

There wasn't enough time to dwell on it, however. Buzz was waving frantically at her to come back inside, which meant the commercial break was over and it was time for the invitation ceremony. The only good thing about that was that she would have the satisfaction of listening to Jenna gasp when yet again she received a green card.

"Minnie Mouse, my ass."

Then there would be Richard's reaction. In truth, she had no idea how he was going to react. But she couldn't wait to find out.

HE GLANCED at the card that Bridget still held in her hand.

Green.

He simply could not believe it.

The cast and crew had packed up and left already, while he'd been forced to listen to the Mouthwash Boys rave about the new element of drama that had been added to the show. He'd also been forced to agree that the battle brewing between Jenna and Bridget might pull in even more viewers.

While he was yessing them to death, Bridget sat quietly on the sofa, waiting patiently for him to finish with the executives. He'd promised to give her a lift home that evening, a promise he'd made thinking she might want a friend's shoulder to lean on after her rejection.

It seemed his shoulder was no longer needed.

Not once since she'd gotten the green invitation did she look smug in her victory. She just sat there, holding her card, smiling ever so slightly at him when their eyes met. Only he knew it was there, beneath the surface, just waiting to bubble out. This was Bridget after all and no one— no one—knew her better than he did.

As soon as he had escorted Don and Dan out of the house, he made his way back to where she sat on the couch. "All right. Go ahead and do it," he prompted.

She smiled at him serenely and stood up. "Ready to go?"

"You know you want to do it."

"I'm sorry?" she asked, her face a picture of innocence.

He crossed his arms over his chest and waited. "We're not going until you get it off your chest...what little of it there is."

That prompted Bridget to stick her tongue out at him and an explosion of action happened after that. She shot one hip to the left, then to the right. Her hips pushed forward, then back. Her arms swung one way and then another. It wasn't the first time he'd seen it, but it was particularly painful this time.

The Smug Dance.

He never should have taught it to her.

"You...were...wrooong. I was riiight. I wiiin! You looose!"

"Please be careful," he reminded her dryly. "It's been a while since you've gotten to do this dance and I know you've never done it in heels that high."

That stopped her instantly. "You're right. Better take it easy this time."

"I hope you're happy with yourself," he said. He could feel the agitation from the evening creeping over him again. He remembered once more that moment right before Jenna had burst out onto the patio. What would have happened? Would Bridget actually have kissed Brock? "Do you know how it looked tonight with you and him and Jenna?"

"How?"

"Like you really did lure him out onto the patio. The way you were leaning into him, it was...it was..."

"Yes?"

"Disgusting!" he fired at her. The anger he'd held at bay since he'd seen her in a clinch with Brock suddenly was reasserting itself. It should have occurred to him that something as prosaic as a kiss should not enrage him quite so much, but he was too busy being mad at her. "It was like watching some soap opera vixen luring her innocent victim off to bed. His jacket around your shoulders, you leaning into him the way you were. It was a damn tutorial on how to seduce an unwitting man. Let me tell you, Jenna came off looking like a sweet angel compared to you."

He saw her listening intently to his words and was satisfied that he had her attention. It wasn't that he wanted to be so harsh with her, but the truth couldn't be ignored. Brock had been the victim, Jenna had been the defending angel and Bridget had been the villain in their performance tonight.

She stared up at him then, her golden-brown eyes wide and sincere. Eyes that, for the first time, he could see without the interference of her glasses. Raquel had been right to insist on the contact lenses, but he was glad she hadn't opted to go with the colored lenses. Her eyes had a special depth and warmth to them that science couldn't enhance.

"Do you really mean it? I was the evil seductress? And Jenna was the sweet angel?"

"Yes," he told her succinctly but truthfully. "How does that make you feel?"

He was waiting for professions of guilt. He was waiting for her to apologize for her behavior. What he did not expect was her larger-than-life smile and the glow of victory.

"That's so cool!" she shouted, thrusting her arms over her head in obvious joy. "For the first time in my life I'm the bad girl! Don't get me wrong, I never minded being the wallflower. Way too much effort and deception in being a seductress. That was for my sisters. But now that I'm doing this and people actually think I'm sexy and alluring, it's sort of fun."

Fun! *What?* That wasn't supposed to be her reaction, Richard thought frantically. He didn't want her to be thrilled with the idea of being a seductress. If she became accustomed to her new role as a vamp, he was never going to get her back as his assistant. She'd be out there seducing all sorts of men.

"No, it's not fun," he shouted back. "Face it, Bridget, you are not cut out to be sexy!"

As soon as the words left his mouth, he knew they were wrong. He also knew they were untrue if his reaction to the sight of her back every time she turned around was any indication. She'd been as sexy as hell tonight.

He should have let her enjoy the attention a little longer.

He should have told her that when he first saw her, his mouth had dried up and his fingers itched to touch her skin. Bridget didn't have a lot of weaknesses, but after years of having her confidence in her sex appeal beat to hell by her sisters and her mother, he knew it was one area in which she was particularly sensitive.

And now it was too late to take back his thoughtless words. He'd snatched her joy away from her like a sibling stealing a favorite toy. Her smile was fading. The sparkle of victory in her eyes was replaced with a hint of pain.

"I'm sorry," he tried, but he could see that it didn't matter. The words had already penetrated deep. "I didn't mean to say you weren't sexy."

"Oh. Okay." She paused for a second, then asked. "Does that mean you think I am sexy?"

Why was it, he wondered, whenever the word *sex* left her mouth, his heart immediately began to pick up speed and he had to force himself to breathe? For the life of him he couldn't fathom what caused these bursts of panic. He didn't have a problem when any other woman mentioned sex. Just Bridget.

"I think you're..." he began, trying to undo the damage he'd already inflicted. "I think you're...um..."

"Never mind, Richard. It doesn't matter. Let's just go," she said matter-of-factly.

She turned and walked away, but he wasn't ready to end this conversation. He reached for her arm and stopped her in her tracks. The contact with her skin was almost jarring. He could feel the delicacy of her bones beneath his fingers and her soft skin rubbing against his palm as his grip tightened. His hand practically tingled where he touched her.

It wasn't the first time this had happened to him, either. Immediately, a memory formed in his mind. The two of them had been slow dancing at her sister's wedding. He recalled getting overheated and rolling his shirtsleeves above his elbows. When he took her back in his arms, they had touched.

Skin to skin.

He'd felt a tingle then, too. But at the time he had he attributed it to alcohol, the hour, the event, anything but Bridget. Certainly not the contact. He'd never really believed any of that stuff about magic happening when two people touched. But there was no questioning it this time.

The tingle was happening. It was tangible. It was physical.

It was frightening.

He stared down at where his hand completely circled her upper arm. When he lifted his gaze, he saw that her eyes were pinned to the same spot. Fearing he was hurting her, he loosened his grip slightly. But that only allowed him to move his hand ever so slowly up and down her arm. He felt her tremble, but still he didn't remove his hand.

"Richard."

Her soft whisper brought him back to his senses. He stopped the motion of his hand and met her eyes so that he could say what he needed to say. What he should have said from the beginning. That much he owed her.

"You looked great tonight, Bridge."

She smiled gently, but the smile didn't quite reach her eyes. "Thank you."

When she tried to pull away he tightened his grip again and forced her attention back to him.

"No," he tried again. "More than great. You looked...as if you belonged."

She didn't smile, but she wasn't scowling or frowning, either. Richard waited a beat and tried to decipher what was going on behind her new wispy bangs, but couldn't.

So much for knowing his assistant inside and out, he thought. It seemed she still had a few secrets left. Richard couldn't suppress the sudden and powerful urge to know what they were.

"We should go," she said. "We've got a busy day tomorrow at the office."

The spell broken, he released his hold on her and watched as she walked away. In a few strides he caught up with her and before she could open the front door, he reached out and opened it for her. She was stunned—because he wasn't necessarily the gallant kind—and she smiled at him almost shyly.

Then out of habit, he placed his hand on the small of her back to escort her through the door as he would have done with any other date. But as soon as he came into contact with bare skin again, he snatched his hand back.

"Damn it, Bridget! Will you find a back for this dress?" He removed his sport coat and dropped it around her shoulders.

She giggled then. An actual giggle from his Bridget. The sound was so frilly and so feminine he had to look to make sure that somehow during all of this television chaos a mischievous person hadn't come along and switched his Bridget for some other creature. A creature who vaguely resembled a dark-haired pixie.

Then he watched her trip down the front two steps to the walkway, cursing her shoes the whole time, and knew that she was indeed still his Bridget.

5

"YES, MRS. CONNOR, I know what it looked like, but really that was just for the cameras. At least, I can only hope so," Richard added a little dramatically.

He'd been in the middle of tweaking his storyboards for a commercial he was doing for a new client when Bridget's mother had called to discuss her daughter's atrocious behavior the night before. He continued to draw while she talked—lectured actually—occasionally responding to something Mrs. Connor said with a "Hmm" or "You're so right." It was the easiest way to handle her.

Richard considered the storyboard in front of him. Here he was working at his job, listening politely to his assistant's mother and doing his best to get her in trouble as a little payback for her Smug Dance the night before. It was times like these, he considered himself a great multitasker.

His office door opened and he spotted Bridget in her traditional uniform of black slacks with a matching black blouse and black shoes. Only this blouse was silk rather than her usual cotton or polyester blend. He could tell by the way it seemed to shimmer when she moved.

This new look worked with her new hair that she could no longer pull back into any kind of bun or ponytail. When left on its own, it fell freely about her face in soft wisps and Richard liked the way she had to brush her bangs casually out of her eyes.

However, she was back to wearing her thick glasses. In a way he was glad to see them because they reminded him that this was the same girl he'd known before all the craziness with the show began—and she would be the same girl after it was over. If he missed seeing her golden-brown eyes, it was a small price to pay.

Catching her attention, he raised his finger to his lips as a silent command to be quiet and pointed to the speakerphone.

"It's just that I don't understand what she could have been thinking. As devoted to her as you are, even to allow another man to get within ten feet of her is flat-out wrong. That's not how I raised my daughters, Richard."

"Yes, Mrs. Connor, I know," he replied sincerely, even as he smiled triumphantly at Bridget. It seems he was going to have the last laugh after all. "I guess I was a little upset. After all, it did look like she was actually going to let Brock kiss her."

Bridget's jaw dropped in silent outrage. Then her eyes narrowed. "Mother, what are you doing calling Richard?"

There was a brief pause before Bridget's mother spoke. "I called him to see how he was holding up, young lady. And to give you a stern talking-to. I saw that red dress you were wearing on television last night. Were you or were you not aware it had no back?"

Bridget huffed. "Margo wore a dress just like that to Cousin Lori's wedding. In fact, if it's possible, her dress had even less of a back."

"That's different," her mother snapped. "That's who Margo is. She didn't go on television wearing it, and she most certainly did not almost kiss a man when she was seriously involved with someone else. Did you consider poor Richard's feelings even once when you decided to embark on this foolishness?"

Richard glanced up from his drawing at the mention of his name and again smiled.

Smiled in a way that made Bridget want to punch him in the jaw. She thought about the injustice of her mother's tirade and had to bite her tongue to keep from exploding. Margo, she knew, had been known to be *seriously involved* with more than three men at the same time. "Poor Richard" was the one who had gotten her into this mess to begin with. To top it all off, Brock hadn't been trying to kiss her at all. He'd only been trying to steady her on those damn shoes.

"I told you, Mother. Richard was the one who made me do the show in the first place. You want to blame someone, blame him!"

There was an ominous silence in the office, so much so that Richard stopped working and stared down at the speakerphone. Then it came. One terse command. "Pick up."

Shoulders slumped, Bridget walked around Richard's worktable to the credenza behind him and lifted the receiver on the phone, which immediately de-activated the speaker function.

"Yes, mother," she replied while her mother began to lecture her on her tone, her attitude and her behavior. Then she dished out the punishment.

"Mother, you can't make me say twenty Our Fathers. Only a priest can do that." Apparently not. "Fine," Bridget relented even as she rolled her eyes. "Yes, and the Hail Marys, too. Goodbye."

She put down the phone and tried to work through the stab of pain that some of her mother's words had caused. It wasn't the guilt she'd inflicted or even the punishment. It was the fact that she was afraid. Bridget could hear it between her words. Her mother was afraid that Bridget was going to blow a make-believe relationship with Richard, and if she did that, she might never find another man. After all, look how long it had taken Bridget to find him.

"What did she say?"

Bridget looked up and saw her boss standing over her, his expression appraising, as though he knew there was more to the conversation then a bunch of Our Fathers. Sometimes it was to her disadvantage that he knew her so well.

"That I'm really lucky to have found someone like you, who miracles of miracles, seems to like me in return. And that I shouldn't jeopardize this because the odds of it happening again are astronomical," she paraphrased, and winced at the bitterness of her tone. She thought she had long ago learned to dismiss her mother's opinion of her as the unattractive and undesirable one. Apparently not.

He frowned and turned back to his work. "Sorry, Bridge. I thought it was funny when she called. I didn't think..."

"I know. It's okay," she said stopping him in midsentence. It wasn't his fault her mother had no faith in her as a woman and the last thing she wanted was his pity. "It's just the way things are in my family. Funny, isn't it though? For years they've been on my case because I don't do enough to make myself more attractive. I don't wear the right clothes or the right makeup. I don't put myself out there in enough social situations. I'm always slinking off into the shadows. So the one time I do something different—"

"You get twenty Our Fathers."

"And thirty Hail Marys. Do you know how long that's going to take me?"

Richard whistled between his teeth.

"Anyway, I don't care what she said. I'm an adult. What my mother says shouldn't affect me anymore." If only that were true.

Thankfully, Richard didn't contradict her, but he did

add, "You know, you're not the only one who has a family with high expectations."

She considered his words and it occurred to her that he knew her family dynamics inside and out, but she knew very little about his. Of course she knew the basics. His father was a doctor: a heart surgeon, to be precise. His mother used to be a lawyer and was now a Connecticut State Supreme Court judge. His brother was also a lawyer who was currently running for Congress and was married to a chemical biologist making significant breakthroughs in drug research while at the same time raising two daughters, the oldest of whom had a natural aptitude for art.

When Bridget put it together like that, she could see that he had a lot to live up to. Granted, Bridget's sisters were beautiful and sexy—there was no doubt about that. But the biggest professional achievement they'd had was when Shelly was promoted to flight attendant in the first-class section of the plane.

Their goal was merely to marry well.

Then there was Bridget. She had been all about moving up the corporate ladder. Richard had plucked her from the administrative masses at V.I.P. that she'd fallen into after college when she was desperate for a job so that she wouldn't have to move back in with her family. He'd made her his personal assistant, but she knew that ultimately he would be the key to her success. Of course, after three years she was still his personal assistant, only now she was on a stupid TV show.

Yep, she was a ball of corporate fire.

But once Richard had his own agency, all of that would change. They would be real partners, and she planned on making her family address her as Vice President Bridget.

Richard, however, never talked much about what his family thought about his accomplishments. She knew that last year when he'd won an industry award for one of his ad campaigns, he hadn't bothered to tell them. She had been the one to tell his mother when Bridget had called to invite his family to the award ceremony as a surprise.

They hadn't been able to make it, what with their extremely busy schedules.

She hadn't thought much of it then. But suddenly it occurred to her how little she knew about their thoughts for his future. Had he told them of his idea of starting his own advertising firm? Heck, she didn't even know if they knew about his comic-strip hobby. If they did, surely they would be pressuring him to pursue his talent, just as she was.

Or would they?

"You know, Richard, it occurred to me that I asked you to spend the holidays with me and my family..."

"Asked?" he interrupted.

"Asked. Blackmailed. Let's not get picky. What will your family think if you don't come home for Christmas?"

He stared at her hard, looking deep into her eyes as if trying to extract what she was really getting at by her question. And since she did have a hidden agenda—digging deeper into his family dynamics and thereby digging deeper into his psyche—she figured she was pretty much caught.

"Leave it alone, Bridge."

But she didn't want to leave it alone. After three years, it astounded her how little she knew about his background. The first place to start in any person's life was the family. "I don't understand why it's okay for me to talk about my family and share every little annoying thing about them with you, but it's never okay for you to do the same."

"You like to talk about your family and I don't. I'm not a sharer," he said as he erased and re-drew something on the page in front of him.

"You're not a sharer?"

He lifted his head. "No. I'm very closed and deeply private."

"Then how come I know about that time in college when you dressed up as a woman because you lost a bet and ended up stripping on a table in a bar? Much to the displeasure of your girlfriend at the time, I might add, who had brought her parents to that particular establishment to meet you."

"I told you that story?"

"Yes."

Richard paused for a moment. "Okay, so I'm not as private as I thought, but I don't want to talk about my family."

"Fine," Bridget agreed. "We won't talk about your family. Can I just ask one question?"

"One."

"Do any of them know about the comic strip?"

With that he burst out into laughter, a full-throttle laugh that gave Bridget her answer. "I don't understand you. Why would you keep that from them?"

"Why do you care?" he asked evidently annoyed by her question.

"Because you need someone to bully you into doing something with that strip and obviously I'm not doing a very good job or else it wouldn't still be in your desk drawer. Mothers make great bullies. Trust me on this. I'm an expert."

"Bridget, trust me when I tell you my family would not approve of me pursuing a dream to become a comic-strip writer and artist. They barely approved of my decision to go into advertising."

That was an interesting piece of information. "Why not? Advertising is a fine profession. And you've been very successful with it."

"Ah, but it isn't noble," he quickly added in a manner that told her he'd received a similar response one or two times before.

She frowned then, and thought about some of the amazing work he'd done over the years in the field of advertising. He'd won not just the one award last year, but also two before that. She thought again about the comic strip he kept shoved in a drawer, except for those she'd managed to steal from him and frame. One she kept over her desk in the corner of his office. The others she knew were mounted on a wall in his apartment. But all of them really belonged to the public. If his family was to blame for that, then they were just as unsupportive as her own. It was a sobering thought.

"It's not right," she said aloud, finding herself truly annoyed with the idea that his family didn't appreciate his gifts. "I'm the only one who ever gets to see what you do. You have this incredible talent and you're wasting it on me."

"You like the strip?"

"Of course I like it."

"Then I'm not wasting it," he said, smiling at her.

She felt her face flush slightly, and the warm glow that he'd left her with the night before when he'd said all those nice things about her belonging was back. "You know there are times..."

"I know. I can be really sweet and gushy. It's a shame most of the time I'm not."

"A pity," she concurred.

"Can we change the subject from my family?"

"Coward," she accused him gently.

"Coward? Wasn't I just on the phone with your mother?"

"Playing the role of the victim. That's nowhere near as scary as being the culprit," Bridget informed him. "However, since we seem to be back on the subject of my mother, now we really can change the subject."

Richard took a pad off of his table and thrust it at her. "These are the restaurant locations for the next four dating segments. Buzz already approved them for setup, camera angles and sound. I need you to go and get permission for us to film there."

Bridget glanced down at the list and smiled mischievously. "Which one do I get to go— Ooh, Frankie's is on the list. I love Frankie's."

"I know."

She looked up at him and wondered at his expression. He looked so serious, perhaps even agitated, but she couldn't fathom why. "Can I go there?"

"Whatever," he mumbled, then once again went back to focusing on the pictures in front of him.

Knowing his mood had shifted and knowing that it was times like these that it was best to vacate the premises, Bridget hopped off her stool and headed for the door. "I'm leaving. I'll call once I get permission from all the owners."

"Remind them of the—"

"Free advertising. Yes, yes. I know what I'm doing. Oh, and I won't be back for lunch."

Richard lifted his head. "But it's Wednesday," he told her, obviously upset by her announcement.

Wednesday was the day that she always picked up sandwiches from Morty's around the corner. He usually ordered roast beef on rye. She typically went with turkey and mayo. And they each shared a single pickle. Bridget thought about their ritual and for the first time saw the unspoken intimacy in it. Vaguely, she wondered if other bosses and assistants were doing the same thing in every office in New York.

Somehow, she doubted it.

It wasn't even that they didn't eat lunch together often, but Wednesdays were special because it was more of an event. On any other day of the week they ate while they worked.

But on Wednesdays, Richard would take out the comic strip, show her what he'd drawn, then panic slightly that she would spill a drop of mayo on one of the boxes as she hovered over the material and ate at the same time. On Wednesdays, he would wait anxiously for her opinion and then pretend that it didn't matter to him when she told him he was amazing. For a man with an ego the size of a blimp, those moments of humility were always so endearing to her.

"I was going to try a special today," he added.

She winced at that, feeling guilty for leaving him, but she didn't back down. Maybe the ritual was getting a little too comfortable. Maybe it was time to make things uncomfortable for both of them to see what might happen.

"I know. But Raquel and I have a strategy meeting." She saw his disappointment quickly fade into irritation when he realized why she was leaving him. It truly bothered him that she was doing this. She could see it in his face. But why? "We also need to shop some more. You didn't think I'd be done with one backless dress, did you?"

He actually gulped. "There are going to be more backless dresses?"

"Maybe not backless...but I am going on a date, one-on-one, with America's Heartthrob. I have to look my best."

He scowled then. "You look fine to me."

"Ah, but I'm not dating you."

If possible, his scowl deepened. "What happened to all that stuff about appearances being superficial and makeup as a tool to cover up the soul? You're a hypocrite and a fraud."

"I know. But I got two green cards on TV. You would be

amazed at what that will do to your value system," she teased. Then, when she saw he wasn't laughing, she added, "Hey, I've been cast in the role of the seductress villain now. I need to look the part."

"Fine. Go. But don't come back without everyone's permission," he barked.

"Later," she said as she headed for the door.

"Later," he grumbled to himself as soon as she left. "Later with no roast beef special. No rye bread. And no pickle. What the hell is a man supposed to do without a pickle on a Wednesday? And what does that mean *look the part?* What does a seductress wear anyway?"

Disgusted with himself, Richard threw down his pencil and eraser and sat back on his stool. He was losing it. That was the only explanation. The truth was he should be thrilled for Bridget. Despite what her mother thought, this show was good for her. It was time that she stopped being a wallflower and got to be Cinderella, instead. She'd looked amazing last night and if he let himself, he could still remember what it had felt like to touch her smooth bare back.

And there was the fact that Brock, even though it was beyond Richard's comprehension that the man had the required depth to do so, had discovered Bridget's inner core. He'd seen beyond her plain, antiflashy appearance to the heart of the woman underneath.

There was no reason why they shouldn't go on this date. No reason why they shouldn't get to know each other better. No reason why Brock shouldn't continue to pick Bridget and certainly no reason why she shouldn't be his choice for a wife.

Over his dead body!

Springing into action, Richard got up and headed to the filing cabinet he kept in the corner of his office. In the bottom drawer, he'd saved all of the videos from different soap opera episodes he'd watched while doing research for his choice of heartthrob. He found the tape marked Brock and popped it into the video/TV unit that he kept on his credenza for viewing commercials.

In the end, he'd chosen Brock because he had both the right look and a quality that seemed more sincere than the other actors. Richard felt that when the camera was on Brock, he was being as honest as he knew how to be in the things that he said and did. Richard felt that the quality of honesty would carry over onto the show.

Only now this tape was important for other reasons.

He needed to know what moves this guy made on a date. If he wasn't mistaken, one of the segments was a scene in which the sincere yet unwitting doctor went out on a date with the scheming manipulative nurse. Not only would he get a chance to see how Brock behaved on a TV date, he'd also get a hint of exactly what a female villain was supposed to look like.

Fast-forwarding the tape, he stopped as soon as he saw Brock's wholesome smile flash on the screen and let it play. The man simply oozed genuineness. It must be those damn blue eyes, Richard thought. At that moment the camera swung around and there she was, the evil manipulative nurse. In a dress cut to her navel and a skirt cut to her....

Oh, no. Not his Bridget. There had to be something he could do to stop this train wreck he'd put himself on...her on. That's right. He'd done this to her and now he needed to save her from herself. Sure, she thought she was having fun, but he knew the truth. This show was corrupting her and it was all his fault. What if Brock did choose her? What if, in a moment of weakness, she said yes to marriage? She'd regret the decision for the rest of her life and no doubt blame Richard. Anything he did at this point to save her from Brock and herself, he was only doing for her own good.

And if that was what he wanted, too, then there was no real harm in that was there?

"TELL ME. How goes the plot to seduce your boss?" Raquel asked over a glass of unsweetened iced tea and a salad with no dressing. The two women sat together in a casual New York restaurant on the West Side. Bridget always preferred the atmosphere in any restaurant west of Seventh Avenue.

Except for Frankie's. That was her fancy place. She made Richard take her there every year for her birthday dinner. She couldn't help but be slightly curious as to why he would put it on the list.

"It's not a plot," Bridget corrected her, swallowing a bite of her hamburger first.

"Did you plan to convince Brock to pick you for the show in order to make Richard jealous and maybe get his attention?"

"Yes," she admitted grudgingly. "But it was really more of an experiment. Not so much a plot. I was subconsciously testing the waters. Sniffing the air. Seeing how the wind blew and all that."

"Oh, I see. A subconscious plot."

Sensing her skepticism, Bridget took a French fry off her plate and shoved it in the thin woman's direction. Raquel's eyes grew wide and panicky as she watched the fried, carbohydrate-filled, salt-covered fry get closer and closer to her mouth.

"Stop it, stop it!" she finally begged. "Take it back. I'm sorry. It's not a plot. Merely a testing of the waters."

Satisfied, Bridget turned the fry around and popped it into her mouth.

"You can be cruel," Raquel informed her.

"I'm in training to be the villain. Speaking of which,

how exactly does the villainous tramp behave? Do I have to slap people?"

"Occasionally," Raquel informed her. "But only at the most climactic moments."

Bridget ate another fry as she absorbed Raquel's knowledge on the subject. "What else?"

Raquel rested her elbows on the table and put her chin in her palm in a pose of deep thought. "Well, she's always manipulating everything and everyone around her."

"Okay."

"For instance, when a man's involved, you want to eliminate your competition."

"You mean you?"

"I'm not really the competition. Jenna is. Besides Lars already told me I'm not allowed to win the next round."

"Got jealous, did he?"

"No, his nail girl in the salon quit and he needs me to start filling in for her during the week. But if I did want to make him jealous, I would get a lot more down and dirty than just doing this show."

Intrigued, Bridget pressed her. "How much more down and dirty?"

Lowering her voice an octave to coincide with her words she said, "Way, way down."

The unfortunate part about not truly being the evil seductress was that Bridget had no idea what that meant or how down was down. "I don't suppose you could give examples. Preferably with diagrams."

"If I did, then you might say that we were...plotting together."

Sensing she'd been outmaneuvered and only mildly surprised by that, Bridget smiled and nodded her head. "Fine. I need help plotting."

Raquel sat up straight and clapped her hands together

excitedly. "If you really want to make someone jealous, you have to think like the seductress. You have to use every trick in the book. The first thing you need to do is to get caught kissing Brock. For real this time."

Bridget considered that and figured that Brock probably could handle one on-air kiss after all she was doing for him. "Okay."

"It has to be a good one. Long and passionate. By doing this you accomplish two objectives—triggering Richard's memory of the time the two of you kissed and inciting his inner beast because you've allowed another man to take his place."

There was one small flaw with that plan, Bridget realized. "I've never kissed Richard."

"Eeeks!" Raquel screeched. "How can that be? I thought you loved him."

"Like him! Maybe like-him like him. Maybe *really* like-him like him, but I didn't say anything about love. I just want to see if...you know...we have anything that might be more than what I thought we had."

The other woman's brow furrowed in sincere confusion. "But you haven't kissed him."

"No. Although there was this one time..."

"Yes?"

"Office Christmas party, a year ago. A little too much champagne and a sprig of mistletoe and..."

"Yes, yes, go on."

"He kissed me on the forehead."

"Ohh," Raquel breathed. "The kiss of death."

"It's not the kiss of death," Bridget responded. Then she thought about how she'd felt more like a little sister than a woman that day. Richard had eventually gone home with Selena from accounting. And she'd gone home. Alone. "Fine. It was the kiss of death."

Slowly Raquel nodded her head. "You have to fix this. Forget my earlier suggestion about kissing Brock. You need to kiss Richard."

"Kiss Richard?" Bridget asked incredulously, already feeling the panic welling up inside her. "As in kiss him? You mean kiss him for real. Kiss him like—"

"Like you love him."

Bridget couldn't stop herself from gulping. Kiss Richard. Her heart was palpitating. Her knees were suddenly knocking together under the table.

Kiss Richard.

It was impossible. Not until she knew how he felt about her. Certainly not until he saw her as a woman rather than just as a valuable assistant. What if he pushed her away? Or worse, laughed at her.

"I can't kiss him," Bridget hissed.

"You have to. How else can you make him green with jealousy if he doesn't even know what he's missing? And how can you know if you lov—like-him like him—unless you kiss him?"

Raquel was right, darn it. The woman was a virtual rocket scientist in matters of the heart, fashion and makeup. Go figure.

"So how do I kiss him? I can't just walk up to him and plant one on him. He'll think I've gone around the bend. Frankly, I'm not too sure I haven't."

"Silly, you're a seductress now. Just do what all seductresses do."

"Tempt him?" Bridget didn't know if that was going to be possible. She'd put everything she had into that red dress and he hadn't been moved to sweep her off her feet. Then she remembered the way he'd touched her arm. He'd stroked her ever so briefly, but it was as if he'd been reluctant to break the contact. At the time, she'd felt a tingling in her arm. She wondered if he had felt it, too. But then, he'd let go of her and it was over. Still, if pressed about the touch, she would have been forced to describe it as a caress. The question was, did she have it in her to entice him to take more?

If so, she was going to need a smaller dress.

"No, silly. Trick him."

This caught Bridget's attention. "What do you mean?"

"Pretend you need him to kiss you for some other reason."

"Like what?" She couldn't wait to hear exactly what reasons a woman had for tricking a man into kissing her.

Raquel held her hands up, palms out, and rocked her head from side to side in consideration. Finally she said, "Like...you've got a piece of gum stuck on your back tooth and you need him to get it...only with his tongue."

Yeah, Bridget wasn't going with that one. Not only would he not buy it, but he more than likely would be grossed out by it. He didn't even like to share a straw with her.

The overall concept, however, did have merit. "I don't know," Bridget fretted. "You don't think it's a little obvious?"

She could see that Raquel didn't understand.

"It's just that every teen movie I ever saw growing up always had a trick kiss in it somewhere. I would like to think that Richard and I were more mature than that."

Of course, he was oblivious to her feelings, which were apparently obvious to the world. She wouldn't share them with him verbally because she was a scaredy-cat. The two of them basically were afraid of their respective families and Richard drew comic strips for entertainment.

So maybe they were not the two most mature people in the city.

"Trick him," Raquel repeated firmly.

Trick him, Bridget repeated silently. It might just work. Then it occurred to her, plotting, tricking... Wow, she truly was becoming the evil seductress. All she had to do was sleep with her sister's husband or abscond with someone else's baby claiming it was hers, and it would pretty much be a done deal.

Richard wasn't going to know what hit him.

BRIDGET STOPPED outside Richard's office door and took a deep breath. She could see him through the beveled glass of the door bent over his drawing table, and considered again the step she was about to take.

What if this backfired? What if she ended up putting all her cards on the table and it turned out he didn't want them? She couldn't imagine working for him after that, but she also couldn't imagine not working for him.

She was his rock. And he was her star. Before her, his career had been in complete chaos. With her, everyone had been able to see through the attitude and recognize his creative genius. Before him, she'd been stuck in a dead-end administrative job, lost in a crowd of secretaries. With him, she was able to use her skills and talents to help land accounts.

They were a team.

But the work was nothing in consideration to all the other things. He wasn't just her boss. He was her friend. He was her confidant. He was her ally in the war against her beautiful family. Until she'd started to think about him differently, romantically, she'd never really considered how much he meant to her.

It frightened her.

A lock of hair dropped over his forehead, which it typically did when he was hunched over the desk like that. It usually meant he needed a haircut, and she would be sure to make the appointment for him sometime next week. For now though, she enjoyed the simple pleasure of watching him struggle to push it out of his eyes while he worked.

When had that happened? she wondered. When did she get to the point that just watching him made her heart ache a little?

It didn't matter. What did matter was that she now recognized her feelings for what they were. Which was all the more reason to go through with her plan, Bridget decided. Raquel was right; she was never going to know if she...liked-him liked him...if she didn't kiss him. As scared as she was about doing this and having it all go wrong, she was more afraid of not trying and then maybe missing out on the most important thing in her life.

Taking another deep breath, she opened the door to his office. He glanced up and grunted, "You're late."

"I got everyone's permission."

"You're still late."

"I brought you back cheesecake," she said holding up a doggie bag.

He eyed the bag and held out his hand for it. "Don't think I can be so easily bribed into forgiving you."

"Okay." But cheesecake always worked on him. She handed over the bag, which had a plastic fork inside and watched him dive into the dessert. Trying to be casual as she figured out a way to work up to her plot, Bridget circled the desk and studied the pictures for the newest print ad they were going to be running for Breathe Better Mouthwash.

He stood back to let her look while he finished off his cake. "What do you think?"

"It's two people kissing." And the best possible opening she could have asked for. Maybe that was a sign.

"That's what single people usually do. Only they do it better with fresh breath."

This was it. It was now or never. "Speaking of kissing, I'm a little worried."

"About what?"

"Well, let's face it, my next time on TV will be with Brock on our date. A date usually implies a good-night kiss at the end of the evening."

"It doesn't have to imply that," he interrupted with a mouthful of cheesecake.

"Surely Brock will want to kiss each of us before he makes his pick for the final two. It's only natural that he would want to find out if he has chemistry with his potential wife."

"Right. Natural." Richard tossed the remainder of the cake in the trash. "So what's the problem? Surely you've kissed someone before."

And why the idea of that would make him nauseous, he wasn't too sure. One thing for sure, she was right about the kiss. He'd watched several episodes of *The Many Days of Life* and in each one Brock was always kissing someone. Passionately kissing, all the time. Usually without his shirt on.

"Of course I've kissed someone before, but never a professional."

That's true, Richard agreed silently. This guy was a professional. The tape was proof. He knew how to angle the woman's head the right way. He knew how to gaze deeply into her eyes right before the moment happened. And after it was over, he always brushed her cheek softly with his knuckles. Why the hell would he do that? More importantly, would Bridget like it?

"Add to the fact that this kiss is going to be shown on TV and I'm really nervous," Bridget continued. "What if I look stupid? You know me. I'm not the most coordinated person in the world. I don't want to do something embarrassing, like bonk noses."

She wouldn't be bonking noses. No sir, not with Mr.

Professional Heartthrob on the case. He would manage the whole event perfectly. And it was driving Richard nuts.

"I think the only answer is to practice," Bridget finished.

Richard shook his head, trying to focus on what she was saying rather than on the image of her and Brock locked in an embrace. "Practice what?"

"Kissing."

"You want to practice kissing Brock?" Oh, this was getting better and better, he thought. Maybe she would want him to videotape it so he could help with their technique.

"I can't practice kissing Brock with Brock," she clarified. "The rules say I'm not allowed to see him outside the boundaries of the show."

That was true. So what in the hell was she talking about?

"If only I knew someone," she sighed and moved around the room aimlessly picking things up then putting them back down again. "A man who would be willing to help me out by just kissing me a few times so I could get back in the rhythm of things."

That statement intrigued him. "How long has it been since you kissed someone?"

"Remember Ryan?"

"Big-tongue Ryan?"

"That's the one," Bridget said, then shivered a little. "Not the greatest last kiss to have logged in one's memory."

Richard conceded that point and thought about the last person he'd kissed. Margaret? No, Marguerite. Or was it just Mary? He couldn't really remember. It hadn't meant anything. It rarely did. A long time ago he'd made a conscious decision to make women a second priority to work. Really, the only woman he'd had in his life consistently was Bridget.

Bridget who wanted to practice-kiss someone.

"So, who are you going to get?" he wanted to know.

"I thought I might ask around the office. Mario is cute and I don't think he's too particular about who he kisses."

"Mario! No way. You're not kissing Mario. You're right. He's not discriminating. You don't know where those lips have been. Besides, he wouldn't let it end with just a few kisses."

"What about Doug?"

"He's got thin lips."

"Evan?"

"He's dating someone."

"Josh."

"Too short." When he realized that made absolutely no sense, he added. "You need someone the same height as Brock so you can practice raising yourself up on your toes. You do realize that's when you will be at your most vulnerable."

"True. So, who do *you* recommend?"

Richard rolled his eyes. He hemmed. He hawed. He thought he had put on a pretty good show if he did say so himself. "I know this is going to sound crazy."

"Yes?"

"What if...now, don't get weird on me or anything...but what if I did it?"

"You?"

"Sure. We're friends. I'm the right height. And I have been told on a number of occasions that I'm a fairly decent kisser." He was getting the panicky feeling back in his chest just at the mention of a kiss, but this time he fought through it. This was for her, after all, and it was the least a good friend could do.

"I was really looking for an off-the-charts kisser."

He scowled at her before he realized she was teasing him. "Naturally, my services don't come free."

"You're going to make me pay you for kissing me?"

"I'll do the Christmas gig, but I was thinking of taking one day off my sentence at the Poconos with your family."

Bridget walked over to him and held out her hand. "Deal."

"Deal," he responded, taking her hand in his and trying not to think about how tiny and slim her hand was and how it fit perfectly into his own. He broke the contact and stepped back. "But we can't do this here."

"No. Not in the office."

"I guess you could come over tonight."

She nodded, a little nervously he thought.

"And you have to bring dinner."

"I just brought you cheesecake."

"Hey. You want access to these lips, you've got to feed me first."

"Fine. Just make sure you have plenty of mouthwash on hand."

Richard eyed the jumbo bottle of Breathe Better Mouthwash on his desk that he used for creative inspiration.

"Not a problem."

6

"YOU'RE NOT STIRRING that right."

Bridget shrugged off the criticism with the ease of someone who'd been told a number of times that she was doing something the wrong way and continued to stir her way. She'd bought pasta, meatballs and sauce from her favorite Italian shop in Brooklyn for dinner. Richard had supplied the wine and the bread.

Leaving the pasta alone for a second she used a spoon to sample the sauce that was simmering in another pot on the stove. She'd told Anthony to go light on the garlic and he'd looked at her as if she'd grown a new head. *Anthony,* he'd told her referring to himself always in the third person, *doesn't do light-on-the-garlic in anything.*

Oh, well, she thought. Good thing they had the mouthwash.

Leaning on the counter next to the stove, a glass of wine perched casually in his hand, Richard peered over her shoulder. "The spaghetti has been cooking too long. It's going to be mushy."

She forked out a single piece and tasted it. Still crunchy. "It's linguine and it needs a few more minutes."

Richard sipped his merlot. "I don't like it mushy."

"Hello, this is me you're talking to. I know you don't like it mushy. Why are you so fidgety?"

"I'm not fidgety," he insisted.

He was fidgety. And he was picky. Picky all by itself didn't mean too much in regard to Richard. He was normally picky about things. But fidgety and picky combined only meant one thing. He was nervous.

He acted this way before he had to do a big presentation for an important account. He would always start those days picking at her over every minute detail and then he'd start to fidget. He'd shove his hands in pockets, then take them out and cross them over his arms. He'd spend minutes fussing with his hair, or tapping pencils on the desk, anything to keep his hands moving.

And if he got really nervous, he'd start pacing. Bridget decided that she wouldn't get nervous herself about tonight unless he started pacing.

The first few times he had exhibited his anxious traits in front of her had happened right after she'd begun working with him. It had almost been grounds for quitting. Or firing, considering that on her second day of working for him, right before a meeting, she had told him to take the stick out of his ass and swallow a chill pill instead.

Amazingly, he hadn't fired her after that episode. And over the course of the next few months, she had begun to see that the criticism wasn't intentional. It was merely his way of deflecting all of his insecurities so he would be confident during the meeting. And the fidgeting was just a by-product of all of his nervous energies. Once she accepted that, it had been easy for her to deal with the minor panic attacks when they occurred.

Only tonight was different. Tonight she was having her own panic attack, which made her decidedly less sensitive to his. In addition to that, his nervousness didn't make sense at all.

Hers, perfectly natural.

She was about to kiss the man who might or might not

be her destiny. That was cause for a little anxiety. He thought he just was helping out a friend. Nothing to be nervous about there. Unless this did mean more to him. Either that or he was really uncomfortable about doing it.

"You know you don't have to kiss me," she blurted out.

He stood up straighter, clutching the glass in his hand. "Why do you say that?"

"It's clearly freaking you out," she stated.

"It's not freaking me out," he answered, totally unconvincingly.

"Fine." Bridget left the stove and picked up her glass of wine. She sat down on one of the stools adjacent to the counter that framed the kitchen and said nothing. For a moment the loft was silent except for the sound of the spaghetti sauce bubbling in the pot, which only seemed to add to the tension.

True to form, Richard began to pace back and forth in the small kitchen. Then in yet another fidgety move, he took the pasta off the stove and poured it into a colander already sitting in the sink.

"That's not going to be done."

He took piece and bit into it. She could almost hear the crunch.

"At least it's not mushy," he allowed. He put his hands on his hips and stared at her hard. "Maybe you're the one freaking out," he finally said. "After all, this was my idea, not yours."

She would have liked to snicker then, taking joy in the fact that she'd really pulled one over on him.

But she was too freaked out.

It didn't make any sense, either. She was a grown woman. She'd had a few relationships in her life. All she was talking about was one experimental kiss. If magic happened, great. If it didn't, she'd find another frog. Either way she would have her answer regarding Richard, and she would be able to move on with her life. Why was it such a big deal?

Because it is, her subconscious answered. She'd always hated it when her parents used that lame answer, and she didn't like it any better coming from her nosy subconscious.

"Maybe we should just do this now." Richard suggested.

Now? Bridget took a large gulp of wine. "Uh, is that chair new?"

Richard glanced at the brown leather recliner that she knew he'd had for years and shook his head.

"Oh. It looks different in this light," she said lamely.

"You're stalling."

"I know," she replied.

They both considered the room as they continued to sip their wine in silence. The Soho loft he rented was spacious with high ceilings. Really, it was one big room that had been sectioned off with different accessories. The counter framed the kitchen in an L -shape. A whitewashed brick wall that ran three quarters of the length of the apartment separated the living area from his bedroom. And another brick wall separated the bedroom from the bathroom beyond it.

The furniture was comfortable, stylish and representative of a man who had done well for himself in Manhattan. Bridget could appreciate the soft leather of the recliner. The sleek lines of the forest-green couch. The coolness of the patterned rug that covered most of the living-room floor. But they weren't her favorite things in the apartment.

Her favorite things were the comic strips he'd written and drawn, his favorite ones—all of which featured Betty—that she'd had framed for him and had threatened death if he didn't hang them somewhere on his walls. Some he'd colored. Some were black and white. All of them were witty, satirical and deeply personal to her.

"Are you backing out?" he finally asked.

No, she wasn't going to back out. She'd come too far to do that. She'd worn a red backless dress, walked in high heels and had succumbed to the evils of makeup. She'd plotted. She'd maneuvered. She'd compromised many, if not all, of her values. Beyond that, she'd gone on TV and flirted with a gay man just to attract Richard's attention.

Now she had it. It was time to act.

Besides it was just a kiss. There couldn't be any real harm in a kiss.

"Definitely not." She took another large swallow of wine, set down her glass and hopped off the stool. "I'm ready if you are."

"I'm ready," he said, chugging down the rest of his wine in several gulps. When he was finished he put the glass on the counter next to hers and looked as though he was considering exactly how to proceed.

"Maybe we should be on the couch."

"But I need to practice on my toes. Then again, I don't really know where I'm going to be when this happens. I suppose we could practice it a few different ways." Very crafty of her, she decided. This way, if she blew the first kiss, she'd already set the stage for round two.

"This isn't some kind of kissing competition between you and the other women," he insisted.

And he really didn't like the fact that she was referring to the first time they were going to kiss as practice. He knew it didn't mean anything. He knew he was only helping her out of a situation he'd gotten her into. Still, they'd known each other a long time and this was new for them. Things were probably going to change after this. They were going to know how the other person tasted. It was completely uncharted territory.

Although there was that one time at the Christmas party.

He'd been drunk on champagne and the success of having been promoted again. She'd stood under a sprig of mistletoe smiling up at him, her face beaming with happiness and, he remembered fondly, pride. Pride wasn't something he'd seen often in the faces of those who were supposed to love him. Seeing it in her eyes, feeling it in his gut, had overwhelmed him with a sense of warmth that he'd never remembered feeling before.

It was so strong that before he realized what was happening, he'd had her face cupped gently in his palms and was bending down to kiss her, until at the last second, some warning deep in his brain shouted out, *Don't go there. Danger. Danger.*

He'd pulled back and instead had kissed her on her forehead. At the time he'd wondered if what he saw in her face was disappointment. But he'd quickly dismissed the idea because he hadn't wanted to consider what it meant if she had been disappointed.

He certainly hadn't acknowledged his own disappointment.

"I'm not trying to compete," Bridget said, refuting his earlier statement and jogging him back to the present.

No, she wouldn't compete, Richard agreed silently. She'd competed too long against sisters to whom she had always lost and the pain of it had left a legacy of deep self-doubt that she managed to hide pretty well. It occurred to him that he should tell her that he could appreciate that particular pain.

Today was the first time he'd talked about his family in any kind of serious way with her. And without dwelling too much on the psychological mumbo jumbo, it had felt good to share. Being considered second class in a first-class family was something he and Bridget could both relate to. Maybe that was what made them such good friends.

Friends who were now going to kiss.

"I know. I shouldn't have said compete," he told her softly. "Come on let's do this thing and get it over with. Then we can eat."

"Okay." She took a few steps closer to him until they stood in front of each other in the center of the room.

He looked down into her eyes and saw her looking back up at him. His heart rate began to pick up speed and his first assumption was that the panic which usually surfaced anytime thoughts of Bridget and sex occurred simultaneously in his head was returning. But in addition to the increased beat of his heart, he felt his gut tighten and his body grow heavier.

This didn't feel like panic. It did feel a lot like desire.

Bending down, he shifted to his right, but she moved left and at the last second his nose bumped against her glasses. Instantly they both tried to change direction, but only managed to bump noses again.

"Maybe you should take off your glasses," Richard suggested.

She laughed self-consciously and reached up to remove her glasses. "Guess I don't need these. It's not like I'm going to have my eyes open anyway."

Her wispy bangs brushed over her forehead and Richard smiled. The haircut was truly flattering and without the presence of her glasses he could see her whole sweet face. He was once again reminded of his pixie—a warm, friendly pixie with big, knowing golden-brown eyes. Even without the glasses he was sure she could see right through him.

"Bridget," he sighed because he wanted to say her name.

This kiss, he decided, their first one, wasn't for practice. This was for him.

He cupped both his hands gently around her face and tilted her head slightly to the side. His lips found hers and he wasn't surprised by how soft they were. He wasn't shocked that they tasted sweet, and wasn't stunned when they opened at his insistence.

It was the most natural thing in the world when her tongue met his and played for a while. In the distance, he heard the thunk of her glasses hitting the floor and then he felt her arms circling his neck. Since he was considerably taller and he was enjoying the warmth and the flavor of her mouth so very much, it only made sense to lift her body up against his so he could have better access and could penetrate deeper.

Naturally, she needed to feel more stable in his hold, so she wrapped her legs around his waist. His hands grabbed her jeans-clad butt to press her even closer against him, forcing the most intimate contact between his hard body and her soft one. Which was fine, he thought dazedly. Everything that was happening was perfectly normal.

Totally natural.

No big deal.

At least, that's what his deluded brain, which he suspected was currently taking orders from a body that had no intention of stopping this unceasing pleasure, kept telling him.

It told him it was okay that he couldn't stop kissing her. No problem that each time their lips separated they reconnected almost instantly, as if they were unable to bear any separation. Who cared that both of them were sacrificing all of their breath just so they could kiss longer, deeper? Air, in his opinion, was highly overrated.

Soon, however, his body, in collaboration with his mind, demanded more. When he carried her into the bedroom, she didn't stop him. When he laid her down on his bed, she reached for his white cotton T-shirt and pulled it over his head. He popped the buttons on her black silk shirt then tossed it behind him and enjoyed the sight of her in white lace.

"You should wear white more often," he murmured, cupping her breasts, which he couldn't believe he'd ever criticized as being small because they were a perfect shape and size for his palm.

His fingers ran over the silky material, at first deliberately missing her nipple until he watched the tiny bud stand firm in a furious bid for his attention. Only then did he tease it between his fingers. Teased it until her back arched like a bow and soft cries escaped from her throat.

"Richard," she sighed. "Please. Please."

Please what? he wondered. Please stop? He hoped not because he couldn't do that. He was a man possessed and the only thing he was capable of right now was sinking himself deep into her body. But first he wanted to taste.

All of her.

His mouth dropped down to the spot where her neck met her shoulder. He nipped at her lightly, loving the resiliency of her flesh over muscle. Then he soothed the tiny mark with this tongue.

On and on his mouth traveled over every inch of her skin, tasting, sucking, consuming her flesh until finally his long lean fingers deftly undid the front clasp of her bra. He stared down at her and watched as her naked breasts spilled free from the confinements. He groaned at the sight of her and his sex tightened painfully against the material of his jeans. Then his mouth was surrounding her breast and the urgency of his swelling erection didn't matter.

None of it mattered, except having her.

He felt her fingers run through his hair and clutch his head to hold him closer and figured that was as good a sign as any that she didn't want him to stop. Then she was reaching for the snap of his jeans. For a moment he lifted his head and looked down their bodies so he could see her fingers freeing him from the buttons, see her hand dip into the opening she created and see her hand grasp his sex, which in all his life he could never remember being so hard or so desperate for a woman's delicate touch.

No, not just any woman. Bridget's touch.

There was so much more he wanted to do to her. He wanted to kiss the back of her knees. He wanted to lick the small of her back. He wanted to taste the very core of her, but her hand was stroking him in a way that was driving him mad. When she squeezed him gently, it was all that he could do to hold on for dear life.

"Bridge, stop. I have to...I need to..."

"Yes," she said, with the infinite understanding that all women seem to have when they realize that a man is at the end of his rope.

She let go of him and the loss of her touch almost made him weep. But then he went to work on her black jeans. The button came loose, the zipper slid down and he pulled the material off her body. Again he took a moment to study the white-lace panties and how they emphasized the pure creaminess of her skin. Then suddenly they were gone.

Without a word, her hands dropped to her panties and she was wiggling the lacy material down over the curve of her hips. The movement of her thrashing body on the bed nearly drove him insane. Finally, she freed herself from all the remnants of her clothes and he did the same, kicking his clothes off desperate to get free of them.

Out of habit, he searched for a condom in the drawer of his night table and sheathed himself before he joined her in the center of the bed where she was waiting for him, her legs open. He fit himself between her thighs and ran his hand down the length of her body. Over her shoulder, over her breast, then a single finger tracing a line down the center of her belly until he found the soft warmth of her sex and sank it deep inside.

"You're so wet," he sighed, his mind reeling at his actions. This was Bridget, he couldn't help but think, and part of him was connected to her. He sank his finger in deeper and knew that he would never have enough of her. She was so wet and tight and nearly delirious with want. He could feel her inner muscles clenching around his single finger, drawing him farther in, even as her thighs worked to close around his thighs.

"Richard!" she screeched, arching her back and thrusting her hips in attempt to take him even deeper. He could see the need expressed in her face, and he knew that no woman had ever wanted him, no, *needed* him like this.

But she was really tight, he realized, and he couldn't take her as hard and as quickly as he wanted without hurting her. Instead, he rolled on to his back and brought her with him, positioning her thighs on either side of his hips. He continued to stroke her with his finger, touching the heart of her to arouse rather than to satisfy. But it was evident she wanted more.

It might have been the fact that she was screaming, "Now, now, now," that gave him his first clue.

Carefully, he lowered her onto his shaft, fighting the need to thrust high and deep inside her. Bridget was in control now, and fortunately, her needs seemed to be magically, wonderfully in tune with his. With her hands planted on his furred chest, she pushed herself down hard and took him all the way inside her until he was lost.

No, he thought, not lost. Found. The word *home* formed in his brain and he couldn't seem to shake it. Each time her wet heat enveloped him, each time her nails sank into his chest, each time she whimpered his name, the word resurfaced. *Home, home, home.* Each thrust of his hips upward sank him deeper and got him closer to it.

Home, home, home.

Harder. Faster. *Home, home.* Deeper. More. *Bridget, home. Bridget, Bridget.* "Bridget!"

He heard her high-pitched cry, felt her body contract around him, knew that the pleasure he felt was being shared, closed his eyes and let himself go.

There was nothing else he could have done.

HOO-KAY, Bridget thought as she collapsed on his chest. That didn't go exactly according to plan. She was sucking in air and trying to come to grips with what had just happened, even though part of her knew she never would. This was supposed to have been an experiment. A simple kiss to see if they had chemistry.

Considering what had happened, she was going to have to go with a big yes on that one.

But what did it mean?

For one, it meant they were good together in bed. Very good. So good. Too good? She wondered if she hadn't killed him he was lying so still. Maybe it would help if she weren't draped over his body. Rolling off him, she fell on to her back. She turned her head toward him and saw one of his arms flung over his eyes, but his chest was moving up and down so he wasn't dead yet. A definite plus.

She wondered what he was thinking, but she wasn't ready to ask yet. Then she wondered what he felt and if it had been a smidgen of what she had. Closing her eyes, she let herself remember the instant of his penetration into her body and she almost whimpered again.

Never before had she felt so completed. Certainly never in her life had she ever let herself go like that. She had never reveled so much in being touched and touching. It had been almost frightening in its intensity.

But not so scary that she didn't want to do it again.

Richard still wasn't moving. And he wasn't speaking. Not a good sign. Someone was going to have to say something. They couldn't continue to lie here on the bed pretending nothing had happened. Especially considering they were naked. But the words wouldn't come. Not the important ones anyway.

The only thing she could think to say was, "Does this mean we can eat now?"

He raised his arm and looked at her, then closed his eyes and moaned.

Yep, definitely not a good sign, she thought. Suddenly feeling very naked, she reached for one of the pillows that had been pushed against the headboard and covered her body with it. Then she scooted over to the other side of the bed and rolled off, not taking into account that her knees were nowhere near ready to support her. She hit the floor with her bottom and emitted a small squeak.

This must have warranted some concern on his part because he rolled over on the bed to check on her.

"What are you doing?"

Bridget stood up, all the while keeping the pillow clutched against her. "I'm not really sure," she told him. "What are you doing?"

He sat up slowly and ran his fingers through his hair. "We can explain this."

"We can?" she asked. Because she didn't think so. She was very much afraid that there was only one explanation for what had happened. At least on her part. Only one reason why she might have fallen into bed with him so eagerly. And if that reason wasn't the same for him, she very much suspected that there was going to be trouble ahead.

Richard rolled off the opposite side of the bed and stood up. Then looking down at himself, he grabbed a pillow, too, and strategically placed it over his thighs. "Things got out of hand," he began.

"Uh-huh."

"We must have been drunk."

"We each had only one glass of wine," she reminded him.

"Strong wine?" he tried.

Bridget could feel the tears welling up, and she knew she wasn't going to be able to stop them. It was right there on his face. The panic. The same look every man got the moment he realized he had let his penis do the thinking for him and, now that it was over, he had to deal with the consequences. Richard wanted to explain their lovemaking as some kind of fluke. The most important thing that had ever happened to her, and he wanted to blame it on the wine.

Bridget began scouring the room for her clothes, which wasn't made any easier without her glasses.

"The important thing," he continued, "is that we don't make too much out of this."

That stopped her in her tracks. "Really?"

"Yes," he said firmly. "It happened. Sure it was a little odd..."

"A little odd?"

Now their lovemaking was odd. She wanted to hit him, but that would have meant dropping the pillow. Bridget found her pants and decided that she really didn't need the panties that went underneath them. What she did need was her shirt.

"As long as we're adults about this, I think everything is going to be fine. I certainly don't think this has to affect our working relationship at all. In fact, in a few days we'll probably laugh about it."

Bridget stopped her search for her shirt and stared at him. Her heart hurt so much she wondered if it might burst. There he was, the idiot, standing naked with a pillow over his crotch, telling her that their working relationship wouldn't be affected by the crazy wild sex they had just shared.

And she loved him.

She was a fool.

Once she found her shirt Bridget scrambled behind the open wall of his bedroom into the bathroom to dress. No bra, no panties, but it didn't matter. She yanked on her jeans and tossed on her shirt only to realize that the top two buttons were missing. Oh, well, she thought a little hysterically, evil seductresses had no problems with a few missing buttons did they?

It didn't matter. She had to get out of his loft and away from him. Now. The last thing she wanted was for him to see her pain, which she knew she wouldn't be able to hide much longer. Glancing down at her feet, she remembered that her slip-on sneakers had fallen off her feet when he'd carried her into the bedroom, so she would have to find them on her way out.

"Bridget, aren't you going to say anything?" he called to her.

She came around the wall, the pillow in her hand and promptly knocked him in the face with it.

"Hey!" he shouted around a mouthful of cotton. "What was that for?"

"That was for being a colossal jerk!"

"I take it we're not going to be adults about this," he said grimly.

"Bite me. Oh, wait, you already did. But don't worry, I'm sure I'll be laughing about it in a few days."

She stormed out of the bedroom and went in search of her shoes. Richard was following behind with his pillow still clutched against his middle.

"Why can't you be reasonable about this?"

Reasonable. What was supposed to have been a simple experimental kiss had turned into earth-shattering, mind-numbing sex and he wanted her to be reasonable. Maybe if she was someone else. Maybe one of her sisters or Jenna could be casual and reasonable at a time like this, but not her. It had meant too much to her. And it obviously hadn't meant anything to him.

She wanted to die. But first, she needed her shoes. Scrambling on the floor, she found the first one and slipped her foot into it. She considered the idea of hopping her way to the subway station on only one foot, but the idea of having a shoeless foot in the subway grossed her out. You never knew what you were going to step in on the floor of that place. In the process of her search she found her glasses and slipped them back on her face.

"Bridget, you have to talk to me about this."

"There's nothing to say." She found the other shoe by the recliner and put it on. She turned back to him then. "Unless you want me to thank you for the practice. Fine. Thank you. But I definitely don't think I'll be needing your services anymore."

Instantly, his face flushed to a deep red hue. Not the kind of red that signaled embarrassment, but the kind of red that signaled real anger. For as long as she'd known Richard, she'd known him to be demanding, arrogant, often moody, but she had never seen him infuriated, and certainly not with her.

He reached out to grab her arms and in the process dropped his pillow. "Take that back," he growled.

Because she was raw inside, because she was feeling just vengeful enough to want to hurt him and because she wasn't really sure what she had said that had made him so mad, she pushed her lips together in a willful act that indicated she had no intention of taking anything back.

"So help me, Bridget, if you're going to consider what happened here as some kind of warm-up for Brock..."

He let the threat hang there, and she was just ornery enough to see where he might take it. "Why not? I wasn't planning on much more than a kiss with him, but at least now I know that if things get out of hand I can measure up to all the soap starlets I'm sure he's had. I did measure up, didn't I? Would you say, on a scale of one to ten, that I was at least a seven?"

She choked on her words and tried to pull herself out of his grip, which only got tighter.

He opened his mouth to say something, then quickly snapped it shut. He took a deep breath and tried again. "Damn it, Bridget. You have to understand something. I didn't...I don't...I can't..."

She didn't want to hear it. She didn't want to know what he didn't or couldn't or wouldn't do. She just wanted to leave.

"Let me go," she demanded. And when he wouldn't, she had to do something she truly despised. "Please," she begged.

He released her then, and she turned and ran for the door.

It slammed behind her with a crash that sounded so damn permanent Richard wanted to break something. His face fell into his hands as he tried to come to grips with what had just happened. Only he couldn't think.

A shower. What he needed was a shower. Then a glass of wine. Maybe some of the bread he'd picked up. The pasta was ruined. He was to blame for that. She'd been right, he had been nervous and fidgety. With very good reason it seemed.

At least he didn't have to worry about the garlic anymore.

The closest thing to him was a vase his mother had given him as a housewarming gift. It was ice-blue and about as emotionally cold as most of his family. He picked it up and sent it flying, enjoying the sound of it crashing against the brick wall and watching as the shards of glass fell silently to the carpet.

He walked straight through the bedroom to his bathroom, not really wanting to remember what had happened on the bed. How intense it had been, how good it had felt, or more importantly, what he might have lost because of it.

Richard stepped into the stall and turned the water on full blast, letting the temporarily cold water punish him. What had he done? And what the hell did she mean about things getting out of hand with Brock?

Shaking his head to try and clear his thoughts, Richard began to understand something about himself and Bridget. It was conceivable that the reason the idea of sex with her had always panicked him was because, deep down, he knew it was going to be just like it was: intense. Not because of any overt sexuality that she could lay claim to or any expertise on his part. The more likely explanation was that their sexual chemistry was born out of a deep and mutual understanding of one another.

Damn it.

He'd been so careful to avoid getting to know a woman on that level. The last thing he wanted or could afford was a real relationship. It wasn't in his plans. Not until he'd reached his goal of making it to the top.

From the beginning of his career, Richard had always been on the success track. More than ever, it was important to stay focused on that track now. He was so close to the top he could almost touch it. A few more weeks, maybe months, and he would have his own advertising agency. With that under his belt he might finally be welcome as a legitimate member of the Wells family.

And wasn't that what he truly wanted? To prove to all

of his family that he wasn't a screw-up anymore. He wasn't the kid who was always staying out late and getting into trouble in high school. He wasn't the son who failed out of Yale in his last year. Or the two-year art-school student. Or the outsider who was always off drawing his "silly little" pictures.

Day in and day out, his mother and his father and his brother had reminded him that he wasn't like them. He was never reaching high enough or going far enough. Not like them. He wasn't saving the world or making laws or protecting the just from the unjust.

He was merely an artist who liked to draw pictures and write some funny lines to go with them. So his whole adult life had been an exercise in reaching a level of success where he could finally turn around and tell his family where they could get off for not loving him because of what he wasn't: one of them.

He lived for the day when he could say to them, "See, you thought I was a screw-up. You thought I wasn't going to make anything of myself. You thought I was an embarrassment. Well, look at me now. And by the way...so long!"

It had been some pretty powerful motivation. Powerful enough for him never to let anything get in his way. Up until now, it had been easy. A naturally self-absorbed guy, he'd been able to block out everything that interfered with his goals. People had been the easiest, since he was more comfortable simply observing them rather than interacting with them.

Women had been even easier. Sex was always simple to get for someone who wasn't grotesque and didn't mind spending the money on a pleasant evening. And relationships were easy to avoid by simply never returning a phone call.

It's not as if he'd been lonely. He had Bridget after all.

Richard turned off the now-tepid water and stepped out of the shower.

For three years she'd been his assistant, his friend, his confidant. For three years she'd grounded his ego while at the same time encouraging his ambition. She'd been proud of his accomplishments in business, but had still pushed him to pursue his comic strip. She didn't think his drawings were silly. She didn't think he was a failure.

And she knew he didn't like his pasta mushy.

When he'd slid into her body and felt her exploding around him, he'd known a sense of peace and welcoming that he'd never experienced before. Not with any woman. Ever. Why did it have to be like that with Bridget—the one woman with whom he couldn't risk getting involved?

Plopping down on the bed, Richard dropped his head into his hands. What was he going to do to fix this? How did they go back to being what they were when they both knew how good this other thing was between them? And how did he pursue his other goal without getting distracted and losing focus on the one thing he'd spent the last ten years working toward?

These were questions that he had no answers for. But all of them paled in comparison to the final question that kept circling around in his head.

What if, God help him, he'd fallen in love with her?

7

"It was very strange. It was almost as if he didn't want to kiss me," Raquel said as she applied a pink-hued blush to the apple of Bridget's cheek. Raquel's date had aired last night, after being taped a few days before. Hers was the second of the four one-on-ones. Bridget's date was to be taped tonight, then finally Jenna's next week. At the end of the broadcast of Jenna's date, Brock would announce the final two contestants live from the Long Island house.

In preparation for tonight's date with Brock, Bridget had willingly agreed to another makeover. Currently, she was sitting at Lars's workstation in his Upper East Side hair studio, allowing herself to be worked over by the two of them simultaneously.

Underneath the extralarge smock Lars had wrapped around her neck, she was already dressed for the date, a blue silk number that floated about her body. It was a dress she'd picked out for herself.

Bridget had been extremely nervous about her non-black choice, as she'd been left to her own devices when Raquel had been suddenly called away from their shopping expedition on a beauty emergency. Bridget hadn't been aware that such emergencies existed until Raquel had explained the dangers of mixing color and gloss. One of Lars's girls apparently had run into trouble trying to find the right combination and Raquel had to race to the rescue to save a bride from the tragic fate of having bad lips on her wedding day.

But today, as soon as she walked into the studio, both Raquel and Lars had oohed at her appearance. Oohs were good. Ohs were bad. That much she had learned from her sisters.

Satisfied with her decision to go with the powder-blue ensemble, she just needed the right hair and makeup to complete the look. Bridget knew that the key to tonight was going to be what she looked like on the outside, since she was currently dying on the inside.

There was no doubt that Richard would be watching, and she had no intention of letting him see what an emotional wreck she had become in the last two weeks. It was one of the reasons why she'd gone with the color blue.

Blue practically screamed emotional stability.

"Ah do not want to hear about theese Brock," Lars exclaimed, noticeably bristling at Raquel's comments regarding Brock. "Ah am very angry weeth you."

Angry was not good. Not when he was snipping at pieces of her hair with razor-sharp scissors, Bridget decided. She thought back to Raquel's statement and felt compelled to intervene on Lars's behalf.

"Why did you kiss him anyway? I thought you were leaving the show?"

"She eese leaving the show. Ah demand it!"

Raquel blew on her brush to expel the excess powder and began to work on Bridget's left cheek. "Oh, hush up, Lars. I don't think Brock will be picking me for the next round anyway. I just wanted to show my audience an on-camera kiss. How you kiss on camera is really important for any actor. Especially if I ever hope to land a lipstick commercial."

"It is?"

"The head must tilt seamlessly."

Unless the man tilted the head for you. Bridget recalled Richard's hands on her face, so gentle but also so firm.

"Your eyes must close on a flutter," Raquel continued.

Bridget wasn't sure how her eyes had closed. There might have been a little fluttering. She had been really nervous.

"The lips must come together like two magnets, practically helpless against the pull."

Yes, that was exactly how she had felt. Helpless. Helpless against the overwhelming surge of need and lust and...love.

The four-letter word forced itself into the front of her brain and she winced. For two weeks she'd been trying to ignore the truth of what had happened, but it wouldn't go away. What had happened between her and Richard hadn't been a kiss gone wild. It wasn't about two sex-starved individuals having fun together after a long dry spell. It certainly wasn't a drunken romp.

It was an explosion of feeling that she'd been suppressing for three years.

She'd very nearly mauled the man. The problem was, she'd been so involved in what was happening to her physically and emotionally that she really hadn't paid much attention to what was happening to him. Looking back on it, it was sort of a blur of lost clothes, naked bodies, soft sighs and rough groans.

She remembered succumbing to his kiss. She recalled throwing herself on him. Then there was the tossing-off-all-her-clothes incident, quickly followed by her lioness impersonation when she'd crawled on top of his body. After that it got a little hazy.

Except for the pleasure.

That was hard to forget. If pressed, she would have bet that he'd been equally pleasured, too. The memory of his body tightening under hers still lingered. And when he had called out her name the sound had been so raw it had sent shivers down her spine.

Yet the instant it was over he had regretted it. Now, everything was ruined.

"But that was the problem with Brock," Raquel explained. "He didn't have any magnets in his lips. He was magnetless." She stood up and studied her work on Bridget's face.

Bridget obligingly looked up at her as Lars ran his hands through her hair in some fluffing motion that, whenever she tried to copy it, made her hair look like a bird's nest. When he did it she looked sexy and tousled. Why was that?

"There you see. The truth eese you cannot be with another man. Only me. That eese why there were no magnets in his lips."

Or the fact that he is gay might have something to do with it, Bridget thought to herself. She almost confided that to Raquel just so her new friend didn't think the lack of chemistry was her fault. But she'd made a promise to Brock to keep his secret and she couldn't break it.

Lars took a step back from Bridget and circled the styling chair. He reached for a strand of Bridget's bangs then twisted and tweaked until finally he nodded with satisfaction. *"Voila. Finis."*

Raquel giggled. "I do love it when he speaks Swedish. Don't you?"

"Always a turn-on," Bridget said, nodding.

Lars frowned and studied her face. "Ah am sensing something eese wrong."

"Nothing's wrong."

Bridget stood and pulled the smock from around her neck. She turned to the mirror amazed again at the difference a little makeup and well-styled hair did for her. All those years she'd fought against fashion and fuss in her personal rebellion against her beautiful sisters. Now she could see that in some ways she'd been not powdering her nose to spite her face.

With her hair feathered about her face and her lips enhanced with the subtle shade of pink, she could almost believe she was pretty. The way the soft blue silk draped around her body, sloping off her shoulders and hugging her curves while at the same time highlighting the good parts, she could almost believe she was sexy.

None of it mattered now. Because the one man she might have wanted to be pretty and sexy for still saw her as nothing more than his assistant, if his comment about them being able to work together was the truth.

An assistant who had become a mistake.

Make that ex-assistant.

Bridget hadn't been to work in the two weeks since it happened. She'd taken the cowardly way out and left a message on his machine at work informing him that she was taking her two-week vacation effective immediately. Then she'd apologized for the short notice, which only served to make her sound pathetic.

He'd called her at least twenty times in that time, leaving messages that very clearly expressed his annoyance with her sudden absence. But she simply couldn't face him, or talk to him for that matter. She couldn't look into his eyes and know that he was wishing that the most incredible night of passion she'd ever experienced had never happened. And what if he figured out that the reason it had happened was because she felt something for him? Something powerful.

He'd probably start being nice to her. Perhaps even going so far as to bring her coffee and doughnuts in the morning. No, she wouldn't have it. She would not let him give her pity coffee or pastries.

Which meant she was going to have to find a new job. Start a new life. Maybe even someday find a nice man...

The tears started running down her cheeks before she even realized what was happening.

"Oh, no! The mascara!" Raquel screeched, immediately reaching for some tissues from the styling counter. She dabbed at Bridget's eyes, catching the stream of black goop as it marked a path down her cheek.

"I'm so...s-s-so-ory," Bridget cried.

"Ah knew it," Lars said. "Did ah not tell you there was something wrong?"

"Hush Lars. Can't you see she is suffering? And on top of it, all her makeup is ruined."

Bridget only cried harder. The two of them pushed her back into the styling chair and continued to press tissues to her face. Raquel did a remarkable job of correcting the damage, but nothing was going to hide her red eyes.

"It's about him, isn't it?" Raquel asked as she finished with the lip gloss.

"Richard?" Lars asked Raquel who bobbed her head dramatically.

"Did you kiss him?" Raquel wanted to know.

Did she kiss him? Let's see there were lips. There were clashing tongues. There were tonsils. Oh, yeah. She'd kissed him. Bridget's head fell forward twice.

"And were there magnets? I mean fireworks? You know, chemistry?" Raquel explained.

Chemistry? She'd been so aroused she'd practically come the second he'd touched her breast. They'd had more chemistry than a periodical chart. H_2Hot.

"You could say that."

"Then everything eese good. *Oui?*" Lars automatically assumed.

"No, everything is not good. Everything is ruined!" Bridget wailed. "It was supposed to be just a practice kiss. Like they do in the movies. The geeky secretary takes off her glasses and the boss realizes she really is beautiful and bang. But then one thing led to another and...and..."

"And?" The couple asked in unison.

"Bang sort of led to boom," Bridget confessed.

They looked at her with equally blank expressions.

"We had sex," she squeaked.

"Mon Dieu!"

"Oh, Lars, no Swedish. Not now. Can't you see how awful this is?"

Bridget glanced warily at Raquel. "It wasn't really awful," she admitted. "In fact, it was really quite good. Amazing in fact. Earth shattering wouldn't be too over the top. I would go so far as to say..."

Raquel shook her head dismissively. "That doesn't matter."

Quickly losing his French/Swedish accent in favor of his native New Jersey tongue, Lars confided to Bridget. "Trust me, it matters."

"No, no. Don't you see, you've thrown the timetable off completely. You needed to start slowly with a kiss to build awareness. But you went for the big bang and the boom-boom and now he's seen you naked. He's probably having a terrible time adjusting."

Bridget wouldn't know that because she refused to talk to him. Besides, the last thing she cared about right now was how *he* was adjusting. She'd been in mental meltdown for two weeks and wasn't showing any signs of recovering. Minute to minute she'd gone from being hopeful to sad to despondent, and back to hopeful again. She'd consumed more ice cream and pizza then any one woman ever should, and she wasn't any more ready to face him than she had been two weeks ago. But tonight, she would. And part of her couldn't wait to see him again.

Fool!

If only she didn't have hope, but the one thing she had learned that night was that they did, in fact, have magnets. No matter how much he might regret what had happened between them, he couldn't deny that the sex had been beyond special.

"I don't know what to do," Bridget finally admitted.

Raquel sighed deeply. "There's only one thing left to do. You can't scheme or manipulate or plot or do any of the good stuff anymore. Now your only option is to...talk."

"Talk?" She couldn't do it. Not to him. Maybe she could send him an e-mail, ask him how things were going. Ask if she still had a job.

"Or you can have sex with him again," Lars tossed in. "That would probably work on me."

Bridget stood up and smiled weakly at her two friends. "I'll figure something out." Later, she thought silently to herself. Much, much later. Maybe sometime next spring. "But right now I need to leave for my date with Brock. Thanks for the hair," she said to Lars.

"But of course," Lars shrugged with the perfect affectation of a New Jersey-born, French/Swedish hairdresser.

"Thanks for the face." Bridget air-kissed Raquel's cheek to avoid smearing her lipstick.

"You really should wear one more often," Raquel told her wisely.

Bridget nodded indulgently, grabbed the shawl and purse she'd bought to go with the dress and left Lars's shop. She opted for a cab to take her to the restaurant where she was meeting Brock rather than the subway. She could never be sure when she was going to burst into tears again and she didn't want to risk a wacko sitting beside her offering his overly used handkerchief.

She stood on a corner and held her hand in the air and watched as blonde after blonde in shorter skirts and tighter halter-tops got picked up before her. Typical. Her sisters never waited for a cab, either.

No doubt that's why Richard regretted what had happened between them. He knew, as the taxi drivers obviously did, that despite the new hairstyle and the new makeup and the decision to wear color every once in a while, she was still just Bridget Connor: quiet, subtle, unassuming...Bridget Connor.

Heck, even she might have regretted sleeping with someone like her.

"Why, if it isn't the competition?"

Startled by the familiar voice, Bridget turned around to find Jenna walking toward her. She was wearing a chic black-and-white striped dress that showed off her amazing cleavage. Her hair flowed over her shoulder and her eyes sparkled, highlighted by a perfect shade of shadow. She was truly a spectacular specimen of womanhood and probably deserved to be on a soap opera.

And she made Bridget feel like her usual plain self. She wished she hadn't worn contact lenses for the date. Right now she would like nothing better than to hide behind her heavy glasses.

"What do you want?" she asked, truly not in the mood to play with the woman today.

Jenna smiled in a way that seemed almost sinister. "I thought you might come here for some beauty advice from Raquel. Oh, and I saw her date with Brock on TV last night. Looks like she won't be making it to the next round I'm afraid. Their kiss wasn't at all convincing."

"Don't worry," Bridget replied, striving for that casual bitch tone Jenna seemed to have mastered. "I won't make the same mistake." Okay, maybe she *was* in the mood to play.

"That's why I'm here. Unbelievable as it is, I think you are my only real competition left on this show. The dark horse candidate that came charging out of nowhere. And when I say horse you know I do mean that literally."

"Cut to the point," Bridget snapped. "I don't want to keep Brock waiting. He said he hates it when I do that."

Jenna's eyes narrowed, but still she managed somehow to hold her smile. "As my competition, it's important that you don't look ridiculously pathetic. So don't even try kissing a professional like Brock. You'll only end up humiliated. Worse, you might trip and end up biting his lip or something."

"I can kiss a man without biting his lip." Bridget thought back to her and Richard. There had been a little biting, but that had really been more nibbling than anything else.

"I've seen you walk in high heels."

Jenna had her there.

"Frankly, I can't wait to make the comparison."

Don't ask. Don't ask. She's setting you up. Don't ask. "What comparison?" *Damn.*

"Why between Richard and Brock, silly. Of course, Richard and I only shared that one kiss on our date before the show started, but he was really rather marvelous."

Bridget felt the air escaping her lungs and tried to stop it. She inhaled and lifted her chin a notch. This wasn't anything new, she told herself. Her sisters always used to do this to her, seducing any boy who ever showed any interest in her. It was as if they had to put her in her place in order to make themselves feel superior. Jenna was just doing the same.

So Jenna and Richard kissed. Big deal.

Even while Bridget was thinking that, her hands clenched into fists and she could hear her knuckles crack. What had Raquel said about the timing of when the evil seductress got to slap people?

Jenna tilted her head at an angle and pushed out her bottom lip. "I'm sorry. Did you not know about me and Richard? If it makes you feel any better, I still say that Brock has to be the more skilled kisser based on his volume of experience. Or maybe not. Tell me, how many girlfriends has Richard had?"

Calmly, Bridget held up her open palm and counted down with her fingers. "Let's see. One, two, three, four, five." On five she glanced down and saw that she had made a fist. Then she came to her senses. She couldn't very well punch the woman in broad daylight.

"Whatever," Jenna said. "Like I said, Minnie, just don't screw up too badly tonight."

Jenna started to walk by Bridget, with her shoulders back, her chin up...so far up, she didn't think to look down at where she was walking. Bridget threw her foot out at the perfect moment and Jenna went tumbling to the city sidewalk. It was truly a beautiful sight to watch.

"You bitch!" the brunette screeched from her current position, which was on her butt.

"Yes, but look at it this way. I've learned what I know about being a bitch from you, so you should be flattered. Oh, and your knee is bleeding a little. You'll probably want to clean that up so it doesn't scar. Bye-bye."

With that she stepped over Jenna's sprawled form and this time when she held out her hand to call for a cab, the cab stopped.

"SO HOW does this work?" Richard asked Buzz. The two men were stationed in a van just outside of Frankie's restaurant in uptown Manhattan. The van was filled with electronic equipment, most of which Richard couldn't recognize and really didn't care about. He just knew that this enabled him to hear what was going on between Brock and Bridget. Something that was of the utmost importance to him.

Buzz groaned a little bit, as if to suggest he really didn't have time to go over this with the ad guy. Richard hadn't felt the need to be on the scene for the first two dates, but that was only because neither of those dates involved Bridget.

Bridget, whom he hadn't seen or talked to in two weeks. Bridget, who had turned his guts inside out and had transformed him into a walking attitude problem. "Buzz," he growled softly. "Trust me when I tell you, you do not want to mess with me today. Now talk."

"We decided to go with a remote approach," Buzz said quickly, evidently taking Richard at his word. "It gives the couple a sense of privacy, but not really. We already arranged with the management what seat they're going to get. Then the couple is rigged with portable mikes so we can catch the conversation. Pete, my second in command, stands outside the restaurant doing the camera work through the window making it seem as if we're eavesdropping on a date, which is what we're doing. I think the barrier adds a sort of noir quality to it. It's almost Hitchcockian."

Great, first Buzz was Spielberg, now Hitchcock. Richard closed his eyes and struggled for patience that he didn't really have. He'd been at the end of his rope since he'd realized that Bridget really wasn't coming back to work. When she'd refused to return his calls, his mood had only darkened. Now, he had to sit here in a van with a wanna-be-serious director to wait for her to show up so he could...

What?

That was a good question. He had no idea what he was going to do or say. He hadn't really known what he was going to say to her on the phone, either. On some level he must have known that Bridget probably wasn't going to take the call, which is why he'd tried in the first place. But things were beginning to get out of hand. He was seriously starting to worry that she might never come back.

Which left him with only one option: full frontal assault. If he could confront her face to face, he was sure that he could convince her to listen to him. As for what he would say, that would simply have to be the truth. That he couldn't get by without her.

He needed her support. He needed her faith in him.

He needed his mail sorted. It was piling up all over his desk and creating chaos in his office.

Not that he was going to start out with the mail thing. He could be dense, but he wasn't that dense. No, the best way to begin was with an apology. She loved it when she thought she was right and he was wrong. She loved it even more when he admitted it.

Bridget, I'm sorry.

That was okay, but it was a little thin. He tried again, silently playing the words in his head.

I'm sorry, Bridge. I didn't mean to...ravish you on my bed to within an inch of your life and mine.

Okay, not exactly what he would call genius. Maybe he shouldn't mention that night at all. Maybe he could get away with playing dumb and simply yelling at her for not showing up to work for two weeks.

What if she quits?

His subconscious prodded him mercilessly with that question. What if she realized that she didn't need him a tenth as much as he needed her and she left him? Then he'd be alone. Alone like he was before her, with only his work and his ambition and his incessant need to prove something to his family. A family who, in the end, he doubted would even care that he'd started his own advertising agency.

None of those things made him smile in the morning like Bridget did. None of those things were inspiration for his comic strip. None of those things really mattered. So why do it?

Because he had to, he thought bitterly. He'd come too far to walk away from it all now. In another few months he'd leave V.I.P Advertising and start his own firm. He'd build his own client list. He'd be a success. A legitimate success with the proof of his name on a door somewhere in Manhattan.

Then he'd tell his family and have the satisfaction of listening to the surprise in their voices when they discovered that little Richie wasn't quite the black sheep they had always believed him to be. They would have to say they were wrong about him. They would have to admit that he did have the stuff it took to be a Wells.

That single dream of proving them wrong had dogged him since the day the Dean of Students at Yale had informed him he wouldn't be welcome back for his senior year due to his low grade point average. His father had pulled all the strings in the world to get him into the school in the first place. Richard had never wanted to go. He'd wanted to go to art school, but art school wasn't a *real* school. The Wells boys only attended real schools. When Richard had got his acceptance letter, his father's only comment was that he doubted Richard would last the first semester.

Being naturally perverse, Richard had worked his butt off for the first year, doing everything he could to keep up in subjects he couldn't care less about. In the beginning he'd managed to squeak by, but after a few years it had caught up to him. In the end, he'd had to tell his parents the bad news and admit that they were right.

"That's all right, son. We didn't think you could do it anyway."
His father's words reverberated in his head, as they

had so often over the past ten years. Usually, every time he thought about slacking off. From the day he'd left Yale, the fantasy of making another kind of phone call to his parents had been his inspiration.

He'd put everything else on hold in pursuit of that dream. No friends, no relationships, nothing. His only distraction was the comic strip, but that was more to unwind than anything else. Nothing had been as important.

Except, here he was sitting in a van waiting for Bridget to show up and maybe for the first time, there was something more important. Someone.

"There she is," Buzz said into the mouthpiece that hung from a headset he wore. Richard looked out the window of the van and saw Buzz's second, Pete, in the street with a mobile over his shoulder calling Bridget to him.

She walked toward him gingerly, no doubt still struggling to walk in her grown-up heels. And from this distance he could see that her face was a little flushed. Tonight she was wearing a blue dress that dipped off the shoulders and slid down over her body in a way that told him the material could only be silk. Suddenly, an image of what she looked like underneath the silk flashed in his head.

Desperately, he tried to shake it loose. He didn't want to remember how smooth her body had been, how the pink tips of her breasts had stood out in wonderful contrast to her white luminescent skin. She was thin. He'd always known that about her. But he hadn't known that she wasn't skinny. He hadn't known that her hips flared with just the right amount of fullness and that her bottom was more than a perfect handful.

He hadn't known any of those things before, and he didn't want to know them now. Because if he thought about them for too long, if he dwelled too much on how good it had been, it would be that much more difficult to let it go. Let her go.

And he had to let her go. It was the only way to keep his focus.

But he had no intention of letting her go all the way. That couldn't happen. She was going to have to accept that, while they couldn't be involved emotionally, they could still be friends and/or colleagues.

Would be friends and/or colleagues.

Must be friends and/or colleagues.

And friends and/or colleagues did not *not* return phone calls. Friends and/or colleagues spoke to each other, worked things out and forgave other friends and/or colleagues for being jackasses when necessary.

At least he hoped she did.

Richard lifted himself off the tire well, although his height kept him bent over at the waist. "Wish me luck, Buzz."

"Why?"

"I'm about to ask someone to forgive me." He turned his head toward Buzz. "Do I look forgivable?"

Buzz studied Richard's face. His pause before answering was a little too long. "Don't take it personally. I don't forgive a lot of people."

Great, Richard thought. He left the van and weaved his way through the cars on 56th Street to position himself in front of Bridget. She stopped short when she saw him, then quickly moved around him.

"Bridget, we have to talk."

"I don't want to talk to you," she called back over her shoulder.

He caught up to her and grabbed her by the arm. Immediately her heel slipped off her three-inch sandal and she cursed him. She did, however, turn around. She wouldn't look at him yet, but the fact that she was facing him, he thought, was progress.

"This can't wait."

"Did you kiss Jenna?" she tossed at him.

So that's why she was so flushed. Her eyes were hopping mad and her teeth looked like they were glued shut. This was not going to help win her forgiveness. "It was an innocent little nothing kiss."

"You mean like our innocent little nothing sex?"

"That's not fair."

"Evil villainous bitches don't have to be."

Richard cursed under his breath. It really had been a nothing kiss. He had been taking Jenna home after their dinner. She'd leaned over and kissed him, probably hoping to ensure her spot on the show. He hadn't really been interested, but being a man means never saying no to a beautiful woman who wants to kiss you. It just isn't done. But Jenna was the last thing he wanted to think about or talk about right now.

"I don't want to talk about Jenna. I want to talk about us."

"Well, I don't."

Stubbornly, she crossed her arms over her breasts. The white pashmina shawl she was wearing as protection against the fall chill slipped down over her arms, revealing more of the creamy shoulders that the dress left bare. He thought about what would happen if he bent over and kissed one of those naked shoulders. And because that was his first thought, he was even more surly with her than he might have been.

"You're behaving like a child," he snapped.

She gasped and shut her mouth so hard her teeth clicked.

"What's next, a temper tantrum?" he pushed. "I don't get what the big deal is. Okay, I kissed Jenna. It meant nothing. But that's not the issue here. The issue is the fact that you have been avoiding me for weeks, actual weeks, and I think I know why."

"You do?"

"Yes. You're a little shy about what happened between us. But you shouldn't be."

"I shouldn't?"

"No. So we had sex. So the kiss went a little too far. People do this every day, Bridge, and get over it. Now, I know it's been a while for you..."

Another gasp.

Perhaps that hadn't been the right thing to say. Richard quickly tried to retreat. "What I meant to say is that I know you're not very experienced with these types of situations..."

Her eyes were thinning into a tight straight line as he spoke. Also not a great sign considering the point of this talk was to move them back to the friends and/or colleagues status. But his frustration over the situation was getting the better of him and he could feel himself losing control of his temper. "Damn it, Bridge, I'm not saying anything you don't already know!"

"You're right," she said with a frosty edge.

But he chose to ignore the frosty tone and concentrate on the fact that she was agreeing with him. "Thank you. Now can we stop this nonsense? You need to come back to work. The mail is piling up and you know how I hate that."

"What I should have said was, you're right, I'm not handling this well. And I'm sure people do it and forget about it all the time. But I'm not one of them." She lifted her head and met his eyes. "I can't go back to the office. I can't sit across from you sorting your mail and taking your messages and forget everything that happened. For heaven's sake you saw me naked!"

"And I've already blocked it from my mind," Richard countered, thinking this might ease her concern.

"Well, I'm glad you were able to block my horrible body out of your mind."

"No, no. I didn't mean it like that."

"I know you regret it."

"Of course I regret it. Look at us. You're barely speaking to me. I had to apologize. Not to mention the fact that we're in the middle of...oh, I don't know...just the biggest moment of my career! I should be focusing on that. I should be focusing on the next stage of the ad campaign that I'm going to use to lure Dan and Don to sign on with my new agency. Instead, I'm stuck here dealing with this mess."

"You're right," she said again.

Only this time he was able to pick up on the fact that it wasn't a good "you're right."

"I never meant to be your mess, Richard."

He heard the slight quaver in her voice and winced. This wasn't how this conversation was supposed to go down. At the end of it he'd imagined them both laughing. Maybe even deciding to go out for ice cream.

But she wasn't laughing. And because she wasn't, neither was he.

"Hey Bridget, let's go," Pete called out to her. "Brock's already inside waiting. We need to start taping if we want to get the restaurant segment in before it gets too crowded."

"I need to go. I need to get my microphone."

He'd almost forgotten about the date. The date was the reason all of this had happened. She'd wanted to practice kissing because she planned on kissing Brock. Richard's whole self rebelled against that idea. He knew what could happen with a simple kiss. Sometimes it got out of control. And he'd be damned before she got out of control with Brock.

"Fine. Have your date. We'll discuss this later. One thing though, you're not allowed to kiss Brock."

She was about to turn away from him when his words obviously registered. "Excuse me?"

"You heard me. I can't trust that things won't get out of hand with him the way they did with me. And right now we don't need that extra complication. No kissing."

Bridget closed her eyes and silently counted backward from ten. When she got to zero she still wanted to hit him. So she counted again. This time she didn't want to hit him. She wanted to cry. Not unusual, considering that everything he'd said so far had brought her perilously close to the edge of tears. But without Raquel to fix her face, she couldn't let that happen.

Didn't he know that what had happened between them was special? Couldn't he guess that the reason their kiss had spiraled out of control so quickly was because there were other forces involved? Actually, just one force. The most powerful force of all.

"You fool," she finally murmured.

"Huh?"

"You don't get it," she said, shaking her head. "I didn't get it, either. It wasn't until...and then I thought maybe...then it happened...and I got it. But you still don't get it." She knew she wasn't making any sense. She could see the puzzlement in his expression, but she had no time, or desire, to explain.

"Say that again."

"No. I'm going on my date. I'm kissing Brock. You kissed Jenna. I can kiss Brock. Then I'm going home, typing up my resignation letter and handing it in tomorrow. After the date with Jenna, Brock has to narrow his harem down to two. If I make the cut, I'll be leaving with him on the next phase of this fun, fun game, which I believe is a weekend retreat in the Poconos. After that, I'll serve out my two weeks' notice and you can spend your time looking for my replacement. Goodbye, Richard."

She turned then without looking back and shuffled, as

quickly as her sandals would allow, toward Pete, who was holding up her remote microphone. The cameraman worked quickly and after a few minutes made her say "test, test" a few times into the small mouthpiece. He must have gotten confirmation that everything was working because he nodded affirmatively.

"Okay," Pete told her. "Don't try to tilt your head to talk into the mike. It's good quality and will pick up your voice, no problem. Oh, and don't spill anything on yourself."

Since she was naturally clumsy, as most of her stain-covered clothes would attest to, she had to ask, "Why?"

"'Cause you could electrocute yourself and die."

Good reason. "Right. No spilling."

"Not even the soup," he warned her ominously.

She nodded warily and then left Pete behind as she made her way to the restaurant door. She could see Brock already sitting at the table, which was positioned adjacent to the restaurant's front window. She waved and smiled, and he put down his breadstick to wave back. He really was very handsome, she decided.

It was a shame that he was gay.

"Bridget," Brock called to her as she entered the restaurant.

He stood up, and as she approached the table he leaned forward as if he planned to kiss her cheek. Knowing that Richard was out there somewhere watching, Bridget turned her head at the last second in an attempt to make lip contact. But instead of their lips meeting it was more like his lips and the side of her nose.

He pulled back, obviously a little confused by her behavior, but she just fanned her face with her hand and told him that she was a little nervous. He seemed to buy that and held her seat out for her. She tried to sit delicately, but her knees, which were still a little shaky from her confrontation with Richard, gave out and she ended up falling into the chair with a plop.

"Thank you," she murmured.

Brock pushed her a little closer to the table and took his own seat. "Is everything okay with you?"

"Of course," she lied. "Why wouldn't it be?"

"It's just that you look a little flustered."

"I told you, I'm nervous."

Brock's brow furrowed. "What's to be nervous about? This is the third time you've been on TV. You should be getting used to it. And it's not like this is a real..."

"Shh," Bridget hushed, cutting him off from whatever he was going to say. She pointed to the little black clip-on mouthpiece that was attached to her dress.

"Oh, right. I forgot. Anyway, don't be nervous. I just want to get to know you better. Much better. All the way better," he crooned.

He was laying it on a bit heavy, Bridget realized, to make up for his near gaff. However, she would take it. She needed all the positive male attention she could get tonight. It would erase the ugly scene with Jenna earlier, and it would help to cement the break between her and Richard. He needed to see her romantically with another man—even if that man was gay—not to make him jealous anymore, but to prove to him that she was truly moving on with her life.

A life without Richard.

Slowly, it dawned on her exactly what she'd done by telling him she was leaving. This was it. This was the real end. Raquel had been right when she'd said there was no more plotting left to do. No more tricks left in the bag, which let's face it, wasn't all that packed to begin with.

And talking hadn't helped at all!

They had talked, and he had called what had happened

between them a mess and her a child. There was no fixing that. Her only recourse was to take the moral high road. To quit. To leave him. After all, how hard could it be to find a new job, a new career path, a new boss that she loved working with, a best friend and the love of her life?

Oh my God, she thought. *I'm going to be sick.*

"Bridget, are you sure you're okay?"

"Why do you ask?" She gulped and placed a hand over her rumbling stomach.

"You look a little green. Are you going to puke?"

Not on TV. Please not on TV, she begged her belly. "I'm fine."

"You know I used to play a doctor, and I learned a lot of stuff about sick people."

Bridget stopped herself from rolling her eyes. She didn't think it would be good for her upset stomach. "Really."

"Sure. On most soaps when the woman gets all queasy and green-looking like you just did, then tries to cover it up by saying she's fine, it usually means only one thing."

"What's that?" she asked.

"She's pregnant."

"Heh, heh," she tried to laugh, frantically struggling to remember if Richard had used a condom. She was sure that he had. Mostly sure. "That really only ever happens on TV," she said, trying to convince herself more than Brock.

Just then their waiter approached the table and Bridget noticed that he had a very familiar gait. When she glanced up, she realized he also had a very familiar face. Her queasy stomach was immediately forgotten and her jaw dropped in disbelief.

The waiter smiled down at her and said in a smooth voice, "Hello, my name is Richard and I'll be your waiter tonight. Is there anything I can get you from the bar?"

8

BROCK WAS immediately confused. "Richard? What are you doing...?"

"That's right, sir," Richard said cutting off Brock's question. "My name is Richard and I will be your *waiter* for this evening." To reinforce his point he winked at Brock.

Brock winked back.

Bridget thought the whole thing was completely surreal.

"Would you like something to drink?" Richard asked them again.

"A double martini, straight up, no olives," Bridget ordered. She was going to need it if she had any plans on surviving the night with her sanity intact.

What in the hell did Richard think he was doing? She couldn't help but think that this was some form of punishment he'd cooked up for her leaving him. Perhaps he planned to drop the martini in her lap and electrocute her on tape.

In fact, electrocution actually seemed like the least painless option for the evening.

"I'll have a club soda," Brock ordered. "Got to stay sharp if my date plans on drinking," he joked, winking again at Richard as if to share the joke with him. "You never know when a lady might need a man to help her into bed."

Richard didn't look as though he found the joke very funny.

"I'll be back with your drinks."

As he walked away from the table Bridget sighed in relief. "Maybe we should ask the manager for another waiter," she suggested tentatively. "I don't like the looks of that one."

Brock, apparently thinking she was kidding, shook his head and laughed. "I'm sure Richard, *our waiter*, will work out fine. Hey, if we don't like him, we can always leave him a bad tip." Amused with his own joke, Brock actually giggled.

Funny that no one had ever picked up on the gay thing, Bridget thought curiously. It really was quite obvious with the giggle.

"Forget about the waiter. After all, this date is for us. I need to get to know more about you if we're going to make a marriage work. I want to know the real person inside." Brock reached across the table; his outstretched arm pushed the breadbasket out of the way in an attempt to hold her hand. Either that, or he was going for the butter; it was hard to be sure. Deciding that he was going for her hand, she met him halfway and put her hand in his. He squeezed it with enough pressure to seem sincere. His eyes focused on hers and for a minute she saw how convincing his heartthrob persona could be.

"Tell me about you, Bridget. What were you like as a girl? What was your favorite Christmas gift growing up? What's your biggest secret?"

Let's see. As a girl, she was all mouth and not very cute. He need only ask her mother for verification of that. Her favorite Christmas gift had been a big Barbie head that she could apply makeup to and style the hair until her sister, Beth, took it because she said Bridget didn't know what it meant to make something pretty. That was roughly when the great makeup rebellion had begun. And her biggest secret? Yeah, like she was going to give that up on television.

"I'm sort of a simple girl," she finally muttered.

"No, you're not. Not simple. You're...well, you're like...really...sort of..." Brock's eyes narrowed and his brow furrowed as he seemed to search his repertoire of dialogue to find the appropriate adjective for Bridget.

"Amazing," Richard announced as he reappeared at the table. They both turned to him and he held up the two glasses in his hands. "Amazing that I made it to the table without spilling a drop, isn't it? Here are two club sodas."

Richard put the glasses down in front of each of them.

"I ordered a martini," Bridget reminded him.

"You didn't really want that," he told her.

"Trust me, I really did."

"It's never good to drink on a first date. Got to keep a clear head and all that." She was about to object when he clapped his hands together and asked, "So are we ready for an appetizer?"

It was too much. Bridget simply didn't have the experience or the emotional resources to play this sort of game. "Richard, tell me what you think you're going to accomplish by this?"

"I'm sorry?"

"You know what I mean. What are you doing here?" Bridget growled.

He shrugged in return, feigning a puzzled expression and Bridget was left wondering how she'd gotten herself into such a predicament. Here he was, standing at her table in a too-tight white tuxedo jacket that he'd obviously lifted from a real waiter, on top of a pair of beat-up old blue jeans, asking her what she wanted for an appetizer.

There was a microphone on her chest. A large camera looming outside the window was focused on her. And when the episode aired her entire family would be watching the debacle that was her love life and laughing. Everyone except her mother that is, who once again probably would be sympathizing with Richard and wondering what he ever saw in her.

To top it all off, she didn't even like club soda. It made her nose itch and usually she ended up sneezing after each sip.

She wasn't a pretty sneezer.

What she really needed was a damn martini. How else did a woman cope with going on a date with a gay, ex-soap-opera star for cable TV, while being waited on by her former lover and soon to be ex-boss?

"I think he's here to get our order," Brock said, answering Bridget's earlier question.

Richard focused on her then, and his expression changed. He looked almost serious. Richard never looked serious. He looked sullen, he looked amused, he looked bored and he looked intense. She'd seen angry once, and it wasn't pretty.

When he'd made love to her...he'd actually looked serious then, too, she remembered. Her heart flipped over in her chest, and she held her breath waiting for what he was going to say.

"I didn't mean to hurt you," he began. So sincerely she wanted to believe it.

"Huh?" Brock asked.

"Uh," Richard stumbled. "I mean I didn't mean to hurt you...by recommending the soup."

"You did hurt me," Bridget confessed. Then for the microphone she added. "I like soup."

"You don't want this soup," Richard replied. "It's bad soup. It's curdled. It can get really hot, and it's got all sorts of baggage in it. Like olives. You hate olives."

"I don't like olives, either," Brock added. "Okay. No soup for us then. What do you have to say about the stuffed mushrooms?"

"Fine. I get your point," Bridget told Richard. "No soup for me anymore. I'm over soup."

Richard turned slightly pale at that comment and got down on his knee next to her. "You can't do that. You can't give up...all soup...for good."

"I can if I want to."

Richard shook his head. "You need soup. And you know it."

"You just told me the soup was bad!"

"Yeah," Brock chimed in. "And you still haven't said anything about the mushrooms."

"A *lot* of soup is bad for you," Richard said, ignoring Brock. "But a little soup never hurt anyone. And this soup does have some redeeming qualities."

"Like what?" she wanted to know.

"Like...peas?"

"Oh, no," Brock said. "Peas? I hate peas. And with olives? No that can't be good. Definitely no soup for me."

Bridget shook her head. She heard what Richard was trying to say, but he couldn't have it both ways. "I don't mind the olives so much or the fact that sometimes it's too hot or curdled. And I love the peas. But I want the bowl."

"What's wrong with a cup?" he asked.

She sighed and pressed her hand to his cheek. His face was one of the most precious things in the world to her. Funny how it was only once she'd realized that, that everything else had come undone. "A cup won't satisfy me. Not anymore."

Richard tried to hold her hand to his face, but she slipped it out from under his grasp. She watched as red infused his cheeks and quickly recognized the change in his expression. He stood up and stared down at her.

This time he looked determined. And she had to admit that she previously had never dared to get in his way when he had his determined face on. There was, however, a first time for everything. What he might not realize was that she was equally determined.

"You don't want a cup?"

"I don't."

"So what are you saying? Are you saying you want...stuffed mushrooms?" he asked, pointing to Brock. "You know they're stuffed with breadcrumbs and butter. It's all fluff and no substance."

Brock raised his hand slightly. "Sounds good. I would like an order of the stuffed mushrooms."

Finding herself on unsteady ground, Bridget wasn't really sure what Richard was asking her this time. He couldn't possibly be arrogant enough to believe that one night with him and she would never want anyone else's stuffed mushrooms ever again. Then again, this was Richard.

Sadly, he might actually be right. But she would be damned before she let him know it. "Maybe I do want the mushrooms."

"Oh, that's rich!" he burst out. "I mean...they are very rich. So rich I can't imagine they would agree with you."

"How do I know until I eat one?" she countered, lingering on the word *"eat"* just to drive him a little crazy.

"Boy, all of this talk is really making me hungry," Brock interrupted. "Do you think it might be better if we just skipped to the entrée?"

Richard surveyed her for a moment then slowly shook his head. "I don't believe you. I don't think you want the mushrooms. And I sure as hell don't think you'll eat one."

"Oh, really?"

"Yeah, really." He folded his arms across his chest and smirked. It was the smirk that did it.

Boldly, Bridget turned her focus on Brock. This time she reached across the table and took both of his hands in hers—first she had to remove the butter knife from one of his hands and the roll from the other—squeezed them and looked deeply into his eyes.

"I want you to know, Brock, that even though we haven't known each other for very long—"

"Just a few weeks. Almost a month," Brock explained to Richard before it dawned on him that Richard already knew that.

"And even though we may not have all that much in common, you being a heartthrob and me being...well, me—"

"You're more than just you, Bridget. I told you that. You're amazing," Brock drawled.

"I was the one who said she was amazing," Richard argued, pointing at his chest.

"Hey, are you going to get us the mushrooms or what?" Brock wanted to know.

Then Bridget squeezed Brock's hands again to regain his attention. Like the consummate professional he was, and indicative of a man who had been in several climactic love scenes on television before, he turned back to her and leaned in closer as if listening even harder than he had before.

"What I'm trying to say is that even though this started out as a game show, and even though I never thought anything would come of it, I think...I truly think—"

"Yeah, come on. Spit it out," Richard pushed her.

"I think I might have fallen in love with you."

"You did?" Brock asked, his face a picture of shock.

"You did?" Richard shouted, his bellow incredulous.

"I did," Bridget lied. For a brief moment she wondered if the gods of love would fire down a bolt of lightning at her for playing with words that were supposed to be saved only for the most important people in a woman's life.

Ten, nine, eight...nothing. Either the gods of love didn't

care, or rather, what she had long suspected, they didn't even know who she was.

"CAN YOU IMAGINE our surprise?"

"Yes, Mother," Richard said aloud into the speaker-phone in his office.

"Can you imagine our horror?"

He didn't think it was all that horrible. For anyone other than him, that was. "What was so horrible for you? I'm the one who got dumped for a soap-opera actor."

"That is so typical of you Richard, making jokes at such a crucial time as this, not even realizing the damage you might have done to your brother's campaign. I don't think I have to mention that running for Congress is just the beginning for your brother."

No, she didn't. Walter was always about the next step. If he won this race, he would begin planning his re-election. If he won that, he'd be looking for a higher office. If he won that, he'd consider the presidency. Vaguely, Richard wondered what Walter would do if he ever did become president. There really wasn't anything beyond that for him to aspire to unless he could start traveling to other galaxies. Maybe he would up and vanish in a puff of smoke, having reached the highest level of achievement known to American man.

Richard reached for his pencil and a pad. He began to draw the image that his mind had conjured, making Walter look half human and half smoke. Then he drew the bubble from the smoke's ethereal lips and wrote the words: "Wait, I'm not done yet. I was never president of the glee club. I can do that, too."

"Richard, are you even listening to me?"

"Of course I'm listening, Mother." He wasn't really. Fortunately, he'd heard speeches like this so often in the past, he knew when to interject when appropriate. "I don't know what you want me to say."

"I want you to apologize to your brother for one. If the tabloid shows get a hold of this, who knows what they might run. Plus he can tell you exactly what you need to say if you are questioned by reporters."

Candidate's Brother Shows Up on Popular Dating Show and Has Odd Conversation about Soup and Mushrooms. More to Come at Eleven.

"It wasn't really the stuff of scandals, Mother. I'm sure it will blow over."

"You'd better hope so. For your brother's career. And what about your father and I? Were you even thinking about our reputations?"

No. He'd been thinking about Bridget who didn't like soup and was in love with mushrooms and who still hadn't shown up for work.

"I was thinking about the show, Mother. I was trying to boost the ratings. This ad campaign for Breathe Better—"

"Yes, yes," she cut him off. "I understand the point of the show. You're trying to sell...something. What is it again? Toothpaste?"

"Mouthwash." He was trying to sell mouthwash. So that he could become a major force in the advertising world, with enough clout to open his own agency, and finally be able to prove to his parents that he'd done something with his life against all their expectations.

"Mouthwash," she sighed so that it echoed throughout his entire office. "Really, Richard, when are you going to get a real job? Something meaningful. Something with purpose. Your father and I never should have encouraged your artistic side."

"Encouraged it? You hid my colored pencils when I was ten."

"For good reason," she huffed. "Look where all of this has gotten you. Kicked out of Yale, working for *mouthwash* people, on some ridiculous show playing a waiter and arguing with a soap-opera actor of all things. What was all that about anyway? Who was that girl?"

"Her name was...is Bridget. She used to work for me."

"A plain thing. Pretty enough I suppose. You should tell her that blue really isn't her color."

Richard was about to interject when he heard the door of his office slam shut. He'd been so caught up in the doodle of his brother, he hadn't even seen Bridget come in. Instantly, he felt a bolt of hope soar though his body. She was here. It wasn't completely over yet.

Bridget marched into the office toward his credenza and glared at the speakerphone. "Really, Mom will you stop calling Richard. It's one thing when you thought we were dating, but to tell him that blue isn't my color simply isn't necessary."

"Who is this? To whom am I speaking?"

Bridget covered her mouth with her palm and shot an anxious look toward Richard. "That's not my mother," she whispered.

Richard leaned over and hit the mute button on his speakerphone so that he could still hear his mother, but she couldn't hear him. "No, it's mine. I think we should trade. Yours likes me better."

"Well, yours thinks I'm plain."

"You don't know my mother. For her *plain* is a compliment. *Flashy*, now that would have been an insult."

"Richard. Who was that? Richard are you still there?"

Her imperious tones cut right to the core of him, and, like the obedient child he never really was, he turned off the mute feature. "Yes, Mother, I'm still here. That was someone from another office. Look, I'll apologize to Walter. Okay?"

"And I can assume you won't be making another appearance on that...show."

Richard took a moment to watch Bridget walk to the small table in his office that primarily served as her desk. He saw her pick up her mug, the mug that he'd given her for her first Christmas present as his assistant. It was a stupid red mug with a Christmas wreath on it that said World's Best Secretary. He'd found it next to the other mugs that said World's Best Teacher and World's Best Boss.

When he'd given it to her she had coolly informed him that she was not a secretary. When he asked her what she was, she replied that she was his senior assistant. Since he only had one, he wasn't too sure what the "senior" meant, but he let it slide. Then she had given him her Christmas present. It was the World's Best Boss mug. He'd thought that had been a good sign.

He watched her pocket the mug in the oversize black raincoat she wore. That was not a good sign.

"Yes. You can assume I won't be giving another repeat performance. Goodbye." He hung up before his mother could, and no doubt she was huffing on the other end of the line, not for the first time wondering why he'd never learned any of the manners she'd tried to instill in him.

Bridget turned away from the table toward him but kept her eyes averted. Her jacket shifted a bit and he caught a hint of green sweater beneath it, worn with a pair of black jeans. Curious, he wondered if it had been Raquel or Brock or some one else entirely who was to blame for the sudden infusion of color into her wardrobe.

She still wore her glasses though. What he previously had thought was the most unattractive piece of her wardrobe—the glasses that hid her face from the rest of the world—he once again found very comforting. His Bridget, the one he'd known for three years, wasn't completely gone.

Then she reached into the inside pocket of the raincoat and laid the letter addressed to him on his desk next to the pad where he'd been doodling.

"Funny picture," she indicated with a nod of her head at the doodle by his hand.

"My brother turning into a puff of smoke after he's served his final term as president," he explained.

"I knew he was running for Congress. But he wants to be president, too?"

"He wants to be ruler of the world."

"Ambitious," Bridget concluded correctly.

"Like everyone else in my family."

Bridget nodded. "Isn't it funny? All this time we've known each other and finally I'm finding out all these things about your family."

"No reason to mention them before," he shrugged. She was supposed to be just his assistant. But she had quickly become more than that. He'd never wanted to admit how close she was to him. It was only now that she was leaving that he was beginning to understand and appreciate that.

Damn her.

"I take it you don't get along with your brother?" Bridget questioned him.

"We're about as close as you are with your sisters."

"Ouch."

"Yeah. So what is this?" he wanted to know as he picked up the letter.

"I told you what it was last week."

Her resignation. He wasn't sure why, but he was hoping maybe she had forgotten that part of the conversation about her quitting then going away with Brock to the Poconos. He had hoped that this was an apology note instead.

"If this is about Jenna—" he began to say somewhat desperately.

"It's not. What you did before we...you know...did it...doesn't matter. Did you two—"

Bridget let the question hang, and Richard took that as an encouraging sign. At least she still cared.

"No. She was trying to ensure her spot on show. And I think you know me well enough to know that I don't mix business with pleasure. At least I didn't before we...you know...did it. Besides, don't you think she would have told you if we had?"

"Probably. You should know I tripped her," Bridget rattled off quickly.

"Excuse me?"

"On the street. There was probably bottom bruising. Definitely knee bleeding. Raquel said it was okay."

"Raquel said it was okay to trip Jenna?"

Bridget winced. "Not exactly. She said it was okay to slap her, but only at the most climactic moment. Which it was, but I'm really not a hitter."

"I'll take your word for it," he mused.

"I thought Jenna might say something to you, maybe try to have me thrown off the show, if for no other reason than to eliminate her competition, but I guess she hasn't. Which leads me to believe she's planning on using the incident to her advantage."

Slowly, Richard eased himself off his stool and circled his drawing table. Bridget backed up a step, but she wasn't leaving. "So you tripped Jenna?"

"Yep."

"Because I kissed her."

"More so because she kissed you. And she ticked me off. You know I'm not normally a violent person."

"You locked your sister, Margo, in a closet with a

mouse for four hours after she ruined one of your favorite party dresses. You said she was so traumatized when she finally got out that she needed therapy for a month."

"Okay, other than that incident."

Richard tried not to let himself hope. In truth, he didn't really know what he was hoping for. But that Bridget would be jealous of him kissing another woman seemed important.

"Have you ever gotten violent with any of the other women I've kissed?"

"No!" she shouted in apparent outrage.

"Never done anything remotely sinister?" He saw the guilt in her face before she could even answer. "Ah-hah!"

"Okay," she admitted. "So maybe I deliberately lost a message or two. Or twenty. I only ever did that for your own good. The women you date are Twinkies."

The women he dated *were* Twinkies. He liked them that way. They didn't demand much more than a nice evening out and good sex. And that was the way it had to be. It was the only way it could be if he was going to match his brother's exalted success or exceed his parents' expectations. Not to mention his own.

His expectations.

Richard considered what that meant. He wasn't even sure he knew what his expectations for himself were. For so long he'd only considered his family's standards. His drive had been born out of a need to prove something to them—that he was, in fact, a legitimate member of the Wells clan. That they were wrong about his abilities.

But now he was beginning to question what that would get him. His mother was so disdainful of the product for his new campaign that she had said *mouthwash* as though it were a dirty word. He had to apologize to his brother—for what, he still wasn't sure.

He'd sacrificed so much to get to where he was and still his family rejected his efforts. He hadn't had a serious relationship since...ever. He wasn't married. He didn't have a child. He didn't really have that many friends.

The only things he had were his blasted ambition and Bridget.

Which is why he couldn't let her go. He needed a better reason for her leaving than what had happened between them, and he needed to know why she really had tripped Jenna.

"Bridget why are you leaving?"

"I told you," she insisted.

"You didn't," he argued. He racked his brain trying to recall what her exact words were, but all he could remember was she didn't know...then she understood...and something about a cup not satisfying her.

"Can't you just accept that this is for the best?"

"You mean you running off with Brock? No. I can't accept that. He's the king of the Twinkies. What if he picks you? Are you seriously going to marry him?"

"I don't know," she hedged. "But he did tell me he was definitely picking me to go with him to the Poconos. We're leaving next Friday. Then I guess we'll see."

The pain that shot through his gut was so intense it left him gasping for breath. All he knew was that he had to do something to stop her. Like lightning he reached out and circled her shoulders with his hands, pulling her closer. With his height advantage he loomed over her and he could see her eyes blinking furiously beneath her glasses.

"All this because we slept together?" he whispered harshly.

"Because you regretted it," she whispered back.

"You know what I regret the most now?"

She shook her head furiously.

"Not doing it again," he said just before he brought his mouth crashing down on hers.

He felt her lips under his and he wanted to moan with the pleasure of it. They were full and seemed to fit his as though they were molded for him. But he wanted more. He wanted everything that he'd had the last time. Her taste. Her scent. Her heat.

He opened his mouth, but she fought it. His tongue brushed her bottom lip, but still her lips remained sealed shut. So he moved onto her chin, then the hollow of her neck, breathing her scent there. His lips scraped a path around her neck until he found the spot directly behind her ear. He heard her sigh when he captured her earlobe and thought that nothing else in this world sounded exactly like Bridget letting go.

"Richard, don't," she pleaded.

He could hear the weakness in her voice, and since he truly wasn't the nicest of men, he exploited it. "Tell me you feel the same when Brock kisses you. I dare you."

"I didn't..."

But he wouldn't let her finish. His lips descended on hers again and this time she welcomed him. This time her tongue met his in a furious duel that was almost as out of control as it had been the last time. Her arms circled his waist and he could feel her lift her leg and wrap it around his thigh in an effort to get closer.

Closer. That's what he wanted, too. That's what he needed. His hand searched under the raincoat until he felt the plumpness of her breast through the soft fabric of the green sweater. In a way, touching her so intimately yet with the barrier of her shirt and bra between them was even sexier than being with any other woman totally naked. Why was that?

Because she's important.

The words hung there in his mind even as he tilted his head to kiss her mouth more deeply. She was important. He could admit that. She was his anchor. His home base. His rock. Without her he was lost. Worse he was alone. Which meant he needed to keep her at all costs. What had she said? That she was leaving because he regretted them being together.

It was the truth. He did regret it. Everything had changed after they made love. If they hadn't, she never would have thought of leaving. Still, he could lie. He could tell her that he didn't regret it. They could even be lovers.

Why not, his mind questioned while his hands crawled up under the green sweater to find the smoothness of her bare skin. This time both of his hands cupped her breasts and she gasped into his mouth.

He knew it wasn't the greatest idea to mix business and pleasure. Normally that had been a pretty standard rule for him. But if making love to Bridget over and over again was the only way to hold on to her, then so be it. A man had to make certain sacrifices in his life.

"Don't leave," he said as he reluctantly pulled his lips away from her luscious mouth. He fell to his knees and lifted the green sweater so he could put his lips to her belly and taste the sweetness of her skin there.

"Do you mean that?"

"Totally." He brushed his cheek against her stomach, caressing her smooth skin. He could feel her tremble under his touch and knew that the slight stubble of his afternoon shadow was both tickling and arousing her.

Oh, yeah, he thought. He could do this. He could make love to her over and over again. Experiment with new positions. Watch her blush as he introduced her to new sensations and deeper pleasures than she had ever experienced before in her sheltered wallflower existence.

"I don't understand," she whispered above him. Then she crooned a soft moan when he dipped his tongue into her belly button. "What made you change your mind?"

Richard pulled back so that he could watch as he pushed the material of her sweater up higher and higher. Finally, he revealed a hint of black silk underneath.

She was a puzzle, his Bridget. Colors on the outside, but now the black was worn beneath her clothes. Only this time, the black silk served to seduce rather than to hide. At least it seduced him.

"You're so sexy. Why don't you let everyone see that side of you? Why do you hide it behind your glasses and your clothes?"

"I don't."

"You do. You hide it, but not with me. With me you don't hold back at all. Why is that?" he wondered aloud as his hand cupped the black silk, letting his fingers and his eyes enjoy the sight and the feel of her. Then when he was ready, he would tug down the material and enjoy the taste of her as well. Not yet though. Not until he had his fill of looking.

Briefly, Richard popped his head around her body and considered the closed door to his office. The drawn blinds would be enough to mask their activities, but he wondered if the fact that the door didn't have a lock should persuade him not to take her on his desk. He wanted to. He wanted to take her right on top of her damn resignation letter, he thought somewhat sinisterly.

But before he could make that decision, she was stepping away out of his reach.

"I thought you knew," Bridget said firmly, pushing her sweater back into place.

How could he not know? How could he know her so well, the real her, and not know that the only reason she went wild for him was because she loved him?

"Come back here," he growled.

It was hard to disobey his command when the gleam in his eye was filled with pure sin. Unfortunately, she knew that the answer to her question mattered more than the pleasure to be found in his arms for a few hours.

Not a whole lot more. But enough so that she had to press him. "Not until you tell me why you changed your mind."

Richard got to his feet and pursued her until she felt her back pressing up against his office door. He bent down once and she was able to dodge his kiss. He bent down again and this time he didn't miss. It was so good, she thought. And so easy to forget her question.

Until he muttered against her lips, "Change my mind about what?"

"About us. About this," she murmured back, running her hand through his hair.

"I didn't change my mind," he said as he cupped her bottom in his hands. "I just decided that the best way to keep you was to sleep with you."

He leaned down to kiss her again, but before he could manage it, his words penetrated her desire-hazy brain. With two hands on his shoulders, she pushed with all of her five-foot-two might until he stumbled backward.

"What's the problem?"

"What are you saying? That you plan to sleep with me just to keep me on as your assistant?" He didn't mean to say that. He couldn't possibly mean to say that. But Bridget was watching his face and she could see that he was still trying to fathom what was wrong with that answer.

"I thought this was what you wanted," he shouted back. "The whole bowl of soup."

"Enough with the soup analogies, Richard. You don't get it. This isn't about sex."

"It was a few seconds ago until you ruined it," he snapped. Then he took a deep breath in an attempt to calm the situation. "I'm trying to give you what I thought you wanted."

Jerkily, she clutched the raincoat around her body, needing the protective shield more than anything right now. The mug in her pocket bumped against her leg as a solid reminder of what she was to him. What she always would be.

The worst part of this was she was coming to understand something about him. Something that she didn't think he knew about himself.

"No, you're not. You're not trying to *give* me anything. You're trying to hold on to me because you're afraid that you're going to lose me. Because you know where that leaves you? Alone," she answered for him.

"That's not true."

She didn't believe him. "You are such a coward. That's the only reason you don't want me to leave. You're afraid of having no one. You don't have your family because for whatever reason they don't seem to get you. You don't have friends because you never let yourself make any. And you don't have a lover because you're afraid to give that much of yourself to anyone."

She watched her words cut him. Saw him visibly rebel against what she was trying to say. "I have goals. I have set markers that I need to reach and I can't let anyone get in the way of that. Not even you," he countered. "I can't."

Bridget shrugged in defeat. There was no fighting that. She knew all about family pressures and trying to live up to expectations that were impossible to meet. Hadn't she gone so far as to convince her boss to play her boyfriend so that she could prove once and for all to her family that she was worthy of someone's love?

That really hadn't worked out so well for her.

"Then you need to do what you need to do, Richard. But I can't be your crutch any longer. And the truth is, I can't let you be mine. I have to find my own way. I suggest you do the same."

His expression turned stony as he turned around and grabbed the letter she'd left on his desk. He ripped it into two clean pieces. Then he ripped it again. "Thanks for the advice. You can leave now."

She couldn't stop the tears, but she did her best to control them. She turned around and reached for the door, but stopped before she opened it. Having her back to him made it easier to say what she felt she had to say one last time.

"I think you're an amazing cartoonist. You really should submit your work to a publisher some day."

That said, she opened the door and closed it softly behind her. She waited until she got into the elevator before she let herself break down. She waited until she got home before she let herself wail in agony. And she waited a few days before she forced herself out of bed, forced herself to shower, forced herself to eat and then forced herself to think about what to pack for her trip with Brock.

To say that she wasn't in the mood for a romantic weekend getaway with Brock was probably an understatement, but she convinced herself it was the only way to make her break with Richard final.

Jenna's date, already taped by now, would air next week. The four women were scheduled to meet at the house on the same night for a live announcement of Brock's final two picks, which would be aired as the last five minutes of the show. Then on Friday, if everything went as planned, she and Brock would leave for the Poconos.

The only residual joy she received over the next few days was the advance copy she got from Buzz on Jenna's date. She'd specifically asked for it, curious to see if Jenna would mention the tripping. She laughed out loud when she saw that Jenna had a cane, a support bandage wrapped around her knee, and she was sporting a large white neck brace that she'd covered with an elegant scarf.

Somehow she still managed to look sexy. Hurt, but sexy.

"I didn't want to tell you, but you've forced it out of me, Brock"

"I did? I thought I just asked about your neck?"

"You need to know this before you make your decision about the final two contestants. Bridget Connor is more than a manipulative game player. She's more than a scheming seductress. She is, in fact..."

Bridget could almost hear the *danh, danh, danh* cords of the ominous organ music that always played in the background during the most dramatic moments on soaps.

"...psychotically deranged!"

Let's see. She had made a decision to leave the man she loved behind forever, and instead was planning on going to a lovely cabin in the woods with a gay ex-soap-opera actor.

Psychotically deranged. That was fair.

9

"I DON'T UNDERSTAND. Why did you have to say that you were in love with me?" Brock asked as he paced back and forth in Bridget's tiny Brooklyn apartment.

It was Friday morning and the limo was due to pick them up shortly for their romantic weekend getaway. Despite Jenna's tale of Bridget's mental mania, Brock still had done the predictable thing in the live portion of last night's show and picked her along with Jenna as the two finalists.

Raquel had been tearful and rather eloquent in her parting farewell to Brock and her audience. As for Jenna, she had had to struggle to hide her pleasure in her victory at being chosen as one of the two finalists, since she was still deep in her role as the sympathetic victim.

Bridget had simply tried to keep herself from looking like either a psychotically deranged nutcase or a heartbroken weepy female. Her fear was that the massive smile plastered to her face, held there by the Vaseline Raquel had rubbed on her teeth to keep her lips from closing—made her look a little bit like the Joker.

Either that or Miss America. It was sort of a toss up.

Not that being labeled as mentally deranged by Jenna was such a bad gig, Bridget concluded. Jenna had kept her distance, and Brock actually had seemed slightly more intimidated by her now. And the host, Chuck, hadn't asked her as many ridiculous questions about her feelings for

Brock. Questions she wouldn't have been able to answer given her current ailment: heartbreak.

Plus, it seemed the fact that she was determined to be not exactly stable was a real boon to the ratings. Apparently audiences loved the idea of not knowing what she was going to do next.

Bridget wished that were actually true. Unfortunately, she knew exactly what she was going to do next and none of it made her happy. Not finishing out the show. Not searching the want ads for a new job. Not, not ever seeing Richard again.

Although it didn't seem as though Richard even cared, she thought bitterly. He'd been behind Buzz watching what transpired on the set, but he'd never once made eye contact with her. He certainly hadn't spoken with her. Instead, he'd been too busy shaking Dan's and Don's hands—not that he even knew which one was which without her—and congratulating himself on such a marvelous success.

Naturally Dan and Don couldn't have been happier with the ratings report that they had been given. There was a very good chance that Richard was going to get his wish and bring them over as permanent clients when he started his own agency. He would have everything he wanted then.

And she would have nothing. Not the career she wanted. Not him.

There was something cosmically wrong with that picture. As a rule, she was a much nicer person than he was. She deserved to have better things happen. Plus, she recycled. Even cardboard. He never did that.

"Why couldn't you have just said that you were growing to care for me," Brock continued, clearly still agitated by her declaration two weeks ago.

"I was playing the scene," she tossed out, not really having any idea what that meant. "Going for the greatest emotional impact."

He nodded knowingly, but then he quickly frowned. "Hey, you don't even know what that means. I'm the actor. Remember?"

Bridget tilted her head in acceptance of being caught. "You got me. I didn't exactly plan it. It slipped out."

"Don't you see though, now everything is going to be weird. If I pick you, I'm eventually going to have to break it off. Only now the world thinks you're in love with me, so that's going to make me look like a rat."

"So pick Jenna and break it off with her," Bridget suggested.

"I can't do that. Number one, I can't trust that she would keep my secret."

That much was true. No doubt her first call would be to *Soap Opera Bi-Weekly* to dish the dirt and simultaneously get her name in print.

"And given the fact that you've sort of made her look like the weak and fragile one..."

Bridget couldn't help but smile. "That does give me a warm and cozy feeling inside."

Brock scowled and finished, "It would still make me look like a rat if I broke it off with her. It's bad enough I'm going to have to dump one of you on the last show. To look like a rat with both of you could severely hinder my chances of winning back the hearts and minds of soap-opera watching women everywhere. I don't know what to do."

He threw his hands up in the air and sighed dramatically as if he was really in the middle of a personal crisis. Bridget wanted to shake him. Figuring out who to dump so you could look the least like a rat wasn't a crisis.

Knowing that your heart was shattered and probably irreparably damaged because you'd just chosen to leave the man you love—for reasons that no longer seemed clear or simple—now that was a personal crisis.

Why *had* she left Richard? Why couldn't she have continued to work for him and laugh with him and make love to him? In hindsight, that arrangement really didn't seem so bad.

Because he doesn't love me.

Oh, that's right! She loved him. He needed her so that he would not be alone. Not exactly the same thing.

No, she decided, that probably wasn't going to work in the long run. And no doubt the pain she would suffer after being with him for several years and coming to the realization that he was never going to love her would be much worse than what she was feeling now.

She didn't see how that was possible, but she had to believe it was true. Otherwise she was a colossal fool for giving up what was almost perfect.

"Not to mention my lover was not at all pleased by your declaration. He has a jealous side to him."

"Chuck's the jealous type? He really doesn't seem like it."

"I didn't say my lover was Chuck," Brock hedged.

"Is Chuck your lover?"

"Yes, and he does have a jealous side. Not that you could possibly understand," Brock informed her, insensible of her anguish. He plopped down on the couch next to her and put his legs up on the coffee table.

Richard used to do that, she remembered sadly. On Friday nights, sometimes after an office happy hour, he'd walk her home then follow her upstairs for another beer. He'd plunk down on her couch, steal her remote control—because there was no other word for taking the remote control when a person was a guest in another person's house—and they would fight for several minutes over what movie they could both agree to watch.

They both really liked the old black-and-white romantic comedies.

Bridget groaned and her head fell into her hands. "I'm such an idiot."

"Oh, come on. You're not an idiot." Brock patted her shoulder in what she imagined was supposed to be a comforting gesture.

It didn't help. "No, no, no," she lamented. "I messed it all up. I don't know what I was thinking."

"You got a little carried away. It happens."

Maybe she could use that as her excuse to Richard. *I'm sorry I quit. I'm sorry I left. I'm sorry I called you a coward for not wanting to be alone... I just got a little carried away.* Hopeful, she turned toward Brock. "Do you think he'll forgive me?"

"You mean me."

Bridget replayed her words. "No, I mean him. Richard."

"Richard?" Brock asked clearly confused. "What's he got to do with this?"

She rolled her eyes once she concluded that Brock still thought she was talking about the night at the restaurant. "I'm in love with Richard."

"But you said you were in love with me."

"I only said that to... I don't know why I said it. To make him jealous, to annoy him, to prove to him that he's not the only man in the universe for me, even though secretly I think he is."

"Oh." Brock took a few seconds with that piece of information. "So you're not in love with me?"

"No."

"That's good."

She nodded. "Considering you're gay and you have a lover, yes, it is."

"I was getting a little worried. I know you have a thing for Richard, but I also know that I ooze a lot of personal charm. Sometimes women can't help but be drawn to me."

"You're a real magnet, Brock," Bridget told him. Then she remembered Raquel's comments about his lips being magnetless and decided maybe he didn't ooze as much charm as he thought he did.

"Hey, speaking of my charm," Brock segued as he bounced off the couch. "I brought you a present."

This was surprising. She didn't get a lot of presents from men aside from Richard's Christmas gifts. But she didn't want to think about those. She didn't want think about the mug, or the purple scarf, or the ridiculous sweatshirt he'd given her one year that had a peacock on the front of it and a logo beneath it that read Strut Your Stuff.

Maybe she should pack that. It could get really cold in the Poconos in fall.

Brock walked over to where he had left his carry-on bag by her front door and extracted a brown paper bag from the side pocket. He carried it back to her and sat first before giving it to her.

She reached inside the bag and pulled out an unmarked videotape. "What's this?"

"My greatest moments," Brock told her with a huge grin. "Some really good stuff I did in the early years of *The Many Days of Life* when I was a rebellious teenager bent on seducing and corrupting the mayor's daughter. That was before I went to medical school though."

"Oh."

"Plus, there is some of my later stuff. A few bed scenes. A few I-love-you scenes. Since I thought you were in love with me, I figured you could use those to, you know...be with me in your head."

"Are we back to the psychotically deranged thing?"

"No," he chuckled. "I thought this would help you get over me. But I guess it's not me you need to get over."

"No, it isn't." Bridget set the tape down and leaned back into the couch. Even that seemed to take effort. At this moment, getting over Richard felt as arduous a task as getting over Mount Rushmore. Simply put, she didn't think she could do it.

"He was watching you, you know."

"When?"

"Last night at the house. When you weren't paying attention. Granted most of the time he was ignoring you."

"I know," she said, still hurt by his cold shoulder even though she understood it.

"Like, really ignoring you."

Like, really. Bridget repeated in her mind. Great, she thought facetiously that made her feel much better.

"Like if you were choking on something, I don't think he would perform the Heimlich maneuver on you, ignoring you."

Which meant he'd let her die before acknowledging her existence. That wasn't comforting. "Is there a point to this?"

Brock nodded. "Because when he wasn't ignoring you so hard, he was watching you."

Bridget didn't want to believe that could be true. "He was not."

This time Brock nodded his head in large bobbing sweeps. "He was! You would turn your head for a second and then he'd zoom in on you. At first I thought he was sort of mad at you, the way he stared at you, but then I thought—"

She grabbed and shook his arm. "What? You thought what?"

"You understand as an actor it's one of my jobs to replicate people's emotions with facial expressions and no words."

"Yes. And?"

"If I had to label Richard's facial expression last night I would have to say that he was...sad."

Sad could be good. If he was sad that she was gone. If he was sad that he let her go. Or if he was sad because his heart hurt almost as much as hers did. Sad was the kind of emotion that tended to churn up other deeper emotions. Sad was the kind of feeling that made you realize what was really important in life.

Bridget was all over sad!

"What do you think I should do?" she asked him.

"Tough call. On the one hand, you don't want to be the one to make the first move. On the other hand, you don't want *not* to make the first move and lose your chance with him forever."

"I know that!" an exasperated Bridget shouted. "That's why I'm asking you what I should do."

"I think I can help you," Brock decided. "But I'll need time to think about it."

Having Brock help her with a romantic problem was a little unnerving. After all he was a soap-opera actor and television's solutions to love's challenges were usually a little on the melodramatic side.

All Bridget could hope was that she wasn't going to have to swallow a bottle of pills, fake a pregnancy or pretend to have some tragic accident in which she contracted a mysterious case of amnesia.

"Hey, since we've got time to kill why don't we watch my tape?" Brock suggested.

Then again, forgetting her life at this very moment might not be a bad thing.

"Knock, knock. Can I come in?"

Richard looked up from his blank tablet, the one he'd

been staring at on his drawing table for the past hour and a half. For the first time in his life, he did not have one creative thought in his head. It was too filled with thoughts of Bridget to have room for creativity, he guessed. He hoped this wasn't about to become a pattern.

He saw Raquel poking her head inside his office door and figured he could do with a little distraction. "Come on in, Raquel. What can I do for you?"

Cautiously, she entered the office and closed the door softly behind her. Richard appreciated the length of her black leather miniskirt, which showed off a significant portion of her fabulous legs.

She was definitely a looker, he thought. No one could accuse him of picking ordinary women to be on the show. Each one of them stood out in their own unique way. Whether it was Jenna's perfectly straight dark hair, or Cynthia's ice-blond curly locks, or Roxanne's fabulous physique, or Raquel's legs or Bridget's... Or Bridget.

She was unique in ways he couldn't even classify. But he wasn't going to think about her anymore. He was going to move on with his life just as she'd done with hers.

Yeah, right.

"I wanted to stop by and tell you personally that I have a confession to make. Lars isn't my *ex*-boyfriend. He's my now-boyfriend. I felt you should know."

"Well, thanks, but it doesn't really matter now that you're off the show. Besides, I sort of figured that out on my own."

"I should have known," Raquel nodded. "Both you and Bridget are very clever. She figured it out, too. Right away."

He frowned then because even the mention of her name hurt. "I suppose she told you that she quit her job."

"Yes, she did," Raquel admitted. She looked around the office taking in the various pictures framed on the wall, all of which featured successful ad campaigns Richard had created. All except one picture that is—the picture that hung over Bridget's worktable featuring his cartoon character Betty. Raquel squinted at the picture. "She looked pretty last night. Didn't you think?"

It took Richard a moment to realize who Raquel was talking about. As far as he knew, Betty from the picture looked the same every night. Raquel, he realized, was referring to Bridget.

She had looked different, Richard admitted to himself.

He couldn't tell if it was the silk flower-print skirt paired with the white linen poet's blouse ensemble that she wore, or the way her hair fell about her pixie face in the most perfect wisps. Or maybe it was the fact that she sat a little straighter in her chair. She seemed taller. More...substantial. He also remembered staring at her mouth for periods of time unable to help himself.

"New lipstick?"

"Passion pink. I picked it out for her. And she bought it. Not the sample size, mind you, but the normal size lipstick tube. She's decided that she's going to try to wear makeup more often."

"She doesn't need makeup," he grumbled, picking up his pencil and forcing its tip to the blank sheet of paper. He still had no clue what he was going to do with it, but thought that maybe if it rested on the paper, it might develop a will of its own and begin moving around.

"Of course *you* would say that." Raquel gingerly lifted herself onto the stool that Bridget typically occupied. It wasn't easy considering her skirt didn't have much give to it. After a time she managed to shuffle her bottom on to the stool and lock her high heels over the bottom rung to keep her situated.

Don't ask. Don't ask. She's setting you up. Wait, this was Raquel. No way *is she setting you up.*

"What does that mean?" Richard finally asked her. "Of course *I* would say that."

"Just that you don't care what she looks like."

"Oh," Richard said somewhat deflated. "That is true. I don't care what she looks like."

"Because you love her for the person she is on the inside."

"Excuse me?"

"It is such a shame," Raquel continued as she worked on crossing her legs within the confines of the snug black miniskirt. "What with you loving her and her loving you, but her quitting and being miserable and you sitting in your office here all alone and being miserable. I don't think I understand why you're doing that."

"Back up a second. I love her?" Richard asked totally flabbergasted by the idea.

"That's what I said. You love her."

"No, I'm asking you why you think I love her? I don't love her."

Raquel giggled and pressed her hand against her lips, but still somehow managed not to smudge her lipstick. "Oh, silly. You can't fool a kidder. I mean kid a fooler. I mean fool a fooler?"

"Kid a kidder."

"Right! That. Anyway I *know* you love her."

She *knew* it. How was that possible when he didn't? "How can you tell?"

"You got jealous when Brock picked her the first time," Raquel counted on her fingers. "You let her steal your cherry at the ice-cream parlor that time we all went together. That's a dead giveaway. You always look when she leaves a room. You fell for the practice kiss..."

"You know about the practice kiss?" He couldn't help but squirm a little at that and wonder if Raquel knew how far the practice kiss actually went.

"I sort of encouraged it. It's a standard ploy in the dating game. But admit it, you wouldn't have fallen for it if you hadn't, deep down in the back of your mind, wanted to know what it was like to kiss her."

Since there was no point in not being truthful considering Bridget was already gone, Richard did have to acknowledge the legitimacy of that statement. He had wanted to know what it was like to kiss Bridget. In some way, he'd been unconsciously thinking about it since the night of her sister's wedding. Certainly when she'd suggested it, he hadn't spent a second considering the consequences.

Those consequences had been significant. She was gone. And it hurt. Was this supposed to be love?

"It doesn't feel like love," he announced.

"How do you feel right now?"

Not great, he assessed. "I miss her. I guess I'm sad. I am sad."

"That's part of love. The pain of it."

"Yeah, but when she was here, when she was my assistant and we were just friends, it wasn't like rockets and fireworks all the time."

"What did it feel like then?"

Comfortable. Easy. Familiar. The words formed a specific image in his mind. "Being with her was like being with...family. Only not my family. My family is still waiting for me to get a real job. My family thinks drawing cartoon pictures is a fruitless hobby. My family thinks mouthwash is a four letter word."

"It's not four letters. It's at least one, two, three—"

"They don't approve of what I do," he said simplifying things for her. "I can't meet their expectations." He'd always met Bridget's expectations though. In his work, with his cartoons. Right up until the very end.

"Ooh! Revolution!"

"I'm sorry?"

"I had a revolution."

"Did you win?"

Raquel squinted at him then shook her head slightly. "I understand it all so clearly now."

"A *revelation*," Richard corrected her finally understanding what she meant.

"You had one, too?"

No point in going there. "What did you figure out?"

"You said that when you were with Bridget before she reminded you of family."

"Yeah?"

"You said you were an outcast in your own family because you could never measure up to their expectations of success."

"Keep going," he prompted.

"Bridget is an outcast, too. Only she can never measure up to her family's expectations of beauty and popularity."

None of what she said was wrong, but he didn't see how it mattered. They were two outcasts. So what? "What's this got to do with me being in love with Bridget?"

"Don't you see? Love comes in all different shapes and sizes and it feels different to different people for different reasons. For you, it feels like what you think family is supposed to feel like. Because that's what you have with Bridget. You were both cast out of your families, so together you made your own family. The Richard and Bridget family."

It was as if the floor gave out beneath his feet and he was dropping twenty floors in two seconds. His throat dropped into his stomach. His palms got a little sweaty. And he saw spots in front of his eyes. The truth of Raquel's statement rang so clear in his head that he thought he might faint from the perfection of the pitch.

He loved Bridget. She was his home. She was his family. She cheered for him, she grounded him, she took care of him and she made him feel like a better man than he knew he was.

Of course he loved her!

Richard looked at Raquel, who was studying her nails very intently, with newfound respect. "You're good."

She beamed at him. "I know."

Richard took a deep breath and assessed the situation. Okay. He'd just discovered that he was in love with Bridget. That was good.

However, she was about to leave for a weekend getaway to a house that was filled with every sex trap known to man. Including a hot tub, a refrigerator stocked with champagne and a shower built for two. She was going to this sex-trap house with a heartthrob who, while not being the brightest bulb in the pack, was, in fact, quite handsome. And sensitive.

And just the sort of man a woman might turn to if she was currently upset about another man.

That was bad.

"I have to stop her."

Raquel nodded. "Of course you have to stop her."

Then he remembered the way Bridget had looked at him after he'd ripped up her resignation letter. Right before she left. "I can't. You didn't see the way she looked at me the last time we talked. Like I was dead to her."

"A woman wouldn't look at a man like that, like he was dead to her, if she never loved him in the first place."

"Are you sure about that?"

She made a face that suggested she was insulted by his doubt. "How can you not know that she is in love with you?"

Pretty much the same way he didn't know that he was in love with her, he figured. "She never said anything—"

"A woman shouldn't have to say anything. It should be

there in her actions. Look at all of the things she's done for you," Raquel noted. "She went on a TV show for you. She dressed up for you. She tried to manipulate you into kissing her. She even bought lipstick for you—actually that one was really more my influence, but you see what I'm getting at. Would a woman do all of those things—things she'd never done in her life before—for a man she didn't love?"

"But what if it's Brock she did all that stuff for? Maybe she wasn't lying when she said she loved him."

Raquel scrunched up her face like she'd just taken a bite out of a lemon. "She doesn't love Brock."

"How do know?"

"Other than the fact that she told me she loved you, you mean?"

Richard clenched his teeth together and strove for patience. "That would have been helpful information to have had at the beginning of this conversation."

"Oh."

Still the news was good. Bridget loved him. Of course she loved him. Raquel was right. What woman in her right mind would put up with half of what he'd forced her to do if she wasn't in love? She'd gone on TV for Pete's sake. She'd sat there while a camera zoomed in on her face.

She hated the spotlight. No, she didn't just hate it. She loathed it.

A vivid memory flashed in his mind. He recalled her two single sisters dragging her out onto the dance floor at their older sister's wedding so they could fight to catch the bouquet. She'd struggled. She'd tried to dig her heels in but because she'd worn flats, her shoes mostly slid across the dance floor. Once there, she'd tried to leave, but each sister had grabbed an arm and bullied her into staying put.

Maybe they'd thought they were being funny, or even helpful by forcing Bridget to participate in the ritual. But it had been there on her face, the agony of being singled out in the middle of the room. The idea that all eyes were on her as she once again lost out to her sisters in a competition.

Richard had seen the way her jaw clenched as she lowered her head and tried to make herself seem as inconspicuous as possible in the purple bridesmaid dress she'd been forced to wear. He remembered becoming enraged at her family for forcing her to participate in such a spectacle. And for not even remotely understanding how difficult it was for her to walk down the aisle in the same dress that two of her sisters wore, knowing that comparisons would be made.

He'd walked out onto the dance floor then and removed the two hands that held Bridget in place. Her sisters had given him harsh looks, but at the time he hadn't given a rat's ass about what they thought. He'd taken Bridget's hand and walked with her off the dance floor and out of the room so she could have a chance to regain her composure. As soon as they were clear of the crowd, she'd turned to him and hugged him. So hard he'd thought they might become stuck together.

And in a way they had.

Then he'd gone and asked her to be on TV. She should have slapped him. She should have quit then. Instead she'd taken a seat and let it all happen. For him. All for him.

It was humbling. And it was solid proof. She loved him. He loved her. Now all he had to do was fix what he'd broken.

"What do I do now? How do I get her back?"

"Oh," Raquel sighed. "I don't know. I'm not so good at this part. I think you're beyond the plotting stage. You're more in the truthful confessions stage. Why don't you call her?"

Calling her wasn't good enough. He needed to see her when he told her how he felt. He wanted to let her know in person that she could have the whole bowl of soup and everything else he had to give if she wanted it.

Please, let her want it. Let it not be too late.

"What time was she supposed to leave with Brock?"

Raquel held up her hands and shrugged her shoulders.

Then it occurred to him that he knew the answer to that. Bridget had booked the limo that was picking them up to take them to the cabin. He made his way to her desk and found a manila folder that contained everything related to the Breathe Better Mouthwash campaign, including a brochure for Charlie's Limousine Service.

Richard called them only to learn that the limo hadn't left yet. So he asked that the driver make a stop at his office before heading to Brooklyn. Since it was his signature on the check, they agreed.

"What are you going to do?" Raquel asked, once he'd hung up the phone.

"I'm going to drive over there in the limo and tell her how I feel," Richard explained. And then he was going to pray to any god that would have him that she loved him enough to forgive him for not realizing how he felt about her. Forgive him for forcing her on TV. Forgive him for saying that he regretted making love to her. Man, she had a lot to forgive. This wasn't going to be easy.

"You can't do that."

"Why not?"

"Buzz will be there with the cameras. I don't think this is the kind of thing you want to do on television."

No, he didn't. For one, there was no reason to risk being dumped again on television if he was wrong about her feelings and she really didn't love him. For another, this was a moment that should just be between the two of them. He didn't want to share it with anyone.

"You could wait until they got back," Raquel suggested.

That was not an option. "And let her go away with Brock Brickman for a weekend to an isolated cabin with a hot tub? I don't think so."

"Okay, but I really don't think you have to worry about Brock. I know this is going to sound strange, but I don't get the impression that he...likes women. If you know what I mean."

Richard snickered at that idea. "Yeah, right. Brock Brickman, America's daytime heartthrob is gay. Can we get realistic here for just a second? I need to think of something. If I don't want to have this go down on camera, and I'm not willing to wait until they get back, then there's only one other option."

"Of course," she said and nodded wisely.

Richard glanced at her. "You know what I'm planning to do?

Raquel nodded at first. Then shook her head. "Not a clue."

10

THE VAN with the camera crew arrived at Bridget's apartment before the limo. Buzz spent some time attaching the portable microphones to both Bridget and Brock and explained that he planned to ride in the back of the limo with them with only one camera.

"Okay, here's what I'm looking for in this scene," he directed. "You're both nervous, but you're both excited. The audience should feel your expectations of the night to come. Will they or won't they? That's the question that should run through the audience's mind as they watch you."

Brock was nodding his head and soaking up everything Buzz was saying. Bridget, however, raised her hand. "I'm confused. Isn't this supposed to be a reality TV show? Shouldn't we just be ourselves?"

Both Buzz and Brock chuckled for a minute at her expense.

"Sweetheart," Buzz explained. "This is entertainment. You want to win big in the ratings, you got to give the people what they want. Now, let's talk about how we want to handle the love scene."

There was going to be a love scene? Bridget gulped. She didn't want to do a love scene with Brock. If Richard saw that, then she would have no chance of winning him back. He didn't know that Brock was gay, and he wouldn't know that they were just acting.

"I was thinking maybe a little kissing on the couch. Then you can follow us to the bedroom. We'll do one last kiss in the doorway, and then we'll close the door," Brock tossed out.

Buzz evidently liked the idea. "That's good. I'll do a nice shot panning away from the bedroom door to give everyone the impression that there's something going on behind it."

"But there won't be anything going on behind it," Bridget announced. She turned on Brock and, through clenched teeth, said, "I thought we talked about this."

Brock flashed a fake smile at Buzz, and pulled her away from the cameraman and his crew so they could speak privately. "Of course nothing is going to be happening behind the door. But I do have a reputation as a heartthrob to maintain. I can't let everyone think I didn't get lucky."

"And I can't let anyone think that I did," she whispered back. "What about Richard? You said you were going to help me get him back."

"I will. After the show is over and I'm back on *The Many Days of Life*. My agent is already in negotiations with the producers," he said gleefully.

"You idiot! After the show is over we'll be engaged!"

"That's right," he muttered, clearly just remembering the name of the show he was currently on.

"The only thing to do is for you to pick me and for me to turn you down." And hope that Richard believed her when she told him that she had not had sex with Brock.

"You can't turn me down," Brock insisted. "I can't have the world see me as some kind of pathetic loser. It's bad enough that I'm going to be a rat for breaking it off with you. But given the choice, I would much rather be a rat than a loser. No, you definitely have to say yes, and then I'll break it off with you. I'll just tell the press that you really are unstable. They'll believe that."

So the world would see *her* as the pathetic loser, not to mention unstable. Perfect. But she didn't care about the world so much as she cared about Richard. As long as he knew the truth, then it didn't matter what anyone else thought.

"Fine. But then I'm telling Richard the truth," she decided. "Right now. I'll call him and let him know the situation and that way he'll know that nothing could possibly happen between us."

"You're going to tell Richard that I'm gay? You promised you wouldn't!"

"That was then. But things are getting out of control now. He has to know."

"He has to know that the person he picked as his heartthrob for a major television ad campaign is gay?"

"Yes," she answered a little more uncertainly.

Brock rubbed his chin with his hand. "I never did ask you that first night we talked about this, but who was responsible for doing the background checks on everyone?"

She jerked a thumb at herself.

"You don't think he might be mad at you for missing that piece of information and possibly putting the show, as well as the ad campaign, as well as his entire career, in jeopardy?"

"Possibly," Bridget allowed. More like definitely. That was part of the reason why she had agreed to this charade in the first place.

Brock crossed his arms over his chest and shook his head slowly. "I'm just saying if it was me, and I was trying to win back the man I loved, I don't think getting him mad at me would be the best approach."

Bridget glared at Brock, hating him for being right. "All right. We'll close the door tonight, you'll break it off with me, the press will learn I'm a nutcase and you'll get back on your show. Richard's campaign will be a success and everyone will be happy. But after all that, you have to promise to tell Richard everything. Deal?"

"Deal." They shook on it, then made their way back to Buzz and his crew just as the limo pulled up behind the van. It was long and black and all of the windows were tinted, preventing anyone from seeing inside. The trunk popped open as a signal to them to put their bags inside.

She might have thought that it was a little odd that the driver didn't get out and help them with their bags, but she was too mad at Brock and too nervous wondering how Richard was going to react to the coming events to care.

They all piled into the back of the limo, with Bridget and Brock sitting on the same seat, and Buzz across from them with a camera on his shoulder. Pete and Gerry followed with the van and were monitoring the picture and sound, communicating with Buzz through an earpiece.

The panel that separated the front of the limo from the back slid down halfway, revealing only the back of the driver's head.

Buzz looked over his shoulder at the driver and asked, "You know where we're going?"

"Yep," came the muffled reply from the front.

Buzz turned his head again and stared for a moment at the driver. Then he turned back to Bridget and Brock and smiled. "Oh, yeah. This is going to be good."

"What's going to be good?" Bridget wanted to know.

"Uh...the lighting," Buzz said, pointing to the sunroof on the limo. Then he lifted the camera on his shoulder. "Okay, let's do it."

Bridget forced herself to smile at the camera and wished she'd remembered the Vaseline trick Raquel had taught her.

"Hey, look, champagne." Brock made the discovery when he opened the minibar.

Champagne. That might work even better than Vaseline, Bridget thought.

Brock popped the cork and poured two glasses. Then he lifted his glass slightly. "To Bridget. And our weekend together. I hope it's everything it can be."

She was about to clink her glass with his when the car turned suddenly and tossed Brock off balance. He ended up spilling his glass of champagne into her lap and she tossed her own glass down her blouse.

So much for the champagne.

"Sorry." The apology from the front was muffled.

Bridget couldn't say why, but there was something about that "sorry" that didn't exactly sound sincere.

The drive into the heart of the Pennsylvanian Poconos only took a few hours along Route 80. For Bridget, however, it seemed endless. The fake smiling thing, which she wasn't exactly great at anyway, became increasingly more difficult as her champagne-soaked blouse and skirt dried and grew sticky against her skin. She was never so happy to see anything as she was the lake house that Richard had chosen for the show. The limo pulled up the long dirt driveway to a large two-story log cabin that sat only a few feet away from the lake.

"Wow," Brock remarked as he got out of the car. "Cool digs."

Not how she would have put it, but accurate enough. The cabin was surrounded on three sides by trees that were practically bursting with fall colors. The cool air, the wonderful colors and the calm lake made for an ideal romantic getaway location. She had to give Richard credit. He did have a good eye when it came to romance.

Thinking about him, though, made her smile even harder to fake. She couldn't shake the image of him sitting in front of his TV watching the camera pan away from the closed bedroom door where she and Brock were allegedly steaming up the sheets. How would he react? Would he be angry? Jealous? Hurt? Or worse, would he simply not care?

Brock had said that when Richard looked at her the other night he'd seemed sad. Maybe Brock was misinterpreting sad with indigestion. Richard tended to get that whenever he ate really spicy foods.

"Let's take a walk," Brock suggested.

"Sorry," Bridget told him. "I need to get out of these clothes first."

Brock wiggled his eyebrows and stepped closer to her, circling her waist with his hands. Bridget could feel Buzz zooming in on them with his camera, and it was everything she could do not to shove Brock away.

Remember, she told herself. She was supposed to be a woman in love, at least that was what she had told everyone watching on their one-on-one date.

"I don't have a problem with that," Brock replied to her suggestion of removing her clothes.

She laughed obligingly at the obvious come-on and hoped it sounded flirty. She didn't feel flirty. She felt sticky and a little sick to her stomach that she'd gotten herself into this mess in the first place.

"I need to take a shower. And before you say anything, I definitely prefer to shower alone."

Brock gave her a little salute and backed off. "No problem, babe. I'll be back in a little while and then we can start thinking about our romantic dinner."

"Don't rush on my account. Take as long as you need." Maybe he would get so tired from his walk that he would simply crash on the couch and she could avoid the whole bedroom-door scene completely.

She made her way to the house and saw that the driver

had placed the bags on the steps leading up to the porch. She turned around and saw that he was already back inside the limo, the driver's-side door closing behind him. A second later, the limo pulled away without so much as a goodbye from the driver and Bridget watched her final chance at escape disappear.

Then again, there was always the van. But that was a stick shift. She didn't do so well with those.

Buzz was following Brock on his nature walk, probably figuring that had to be more exciting than watching a closed door while she took a shower. Which meant, at least for the next hour or so, she would be left alone.

She grabbed her overnight bag and made her way into the house. The first thing she noticed was that the furnishings meshed with the ambiance of the log cabin. This place lacked the sophistication of the Long Island house, where they had filmed the group shows. But what it lacked in sophistication it made up for it in cozy. A large brick fireplace was situated in the center of a living area and around it were several large oak chairs covered with brightly colored cushions. The chairs were designed to fit two people. Perfect for snuggling.

The stairs ran along the far left wall. Bridget climbed them to the second floor where she discovered two bedrooms on either side of a narrow hallway. She chose the larger of the two bedrooms, and when her eyes fell to the massive king-size bed, she shuddered.

No doubt Buzz would get a shot of the room before the big scene tonight to give everyone an image of exactly where the deed would be going down. There was no way that Richard would believe nothing happened. Certainly not after hearing her tell Brock that she loved him. And not with a bed that looked so blatantly inviting with the quilted duvet in an array of bright colors and matching thick pillows. It was made for making love on a brisk fall evening in a cabin tucked away in the middle of the woods. If only she could be doing that with Richard instead of faking it with Brock.

Unable to dwell on her dire circumstances any longer, Bridget stripped out of her sticky clothes and headed for the master bath.

RICHARD DROVE the limo down the driveway, turned it onto the dirt road that led back to the highway and parked it. Brock was taking a walk and the cameras were all on him right now, which meant Richard had the chance to catch Bridget alone in the house. But he needed to act fast. He tossed off his cap and suit coat and then jogged back up the driveway. When he got closer to the house, he slowed down and checked for signs of anyone lingering about. He heard voices and saw that Pete and Gerry were still hanging out by the van.

Not wanting to sound any alarms about his presence, he made his way into the woods that surrounded the house and moved from tree to tree. The back of the house had a large deck attached to it in case a person wanted to overlook the woods instead of the lake. As stealthily as he could, he made his way up the stairs to the deck and spotted the back door that led to the kitchen. Having scouted this location himself, he knew that the key to the back door was hidden under the welcome mat by the door.

Richard found the key and used it to let himself inside, and then went in search of Bridget. She wasn't downstairs. He quickly concluded that she had probably wanted to change out of her clothes.

He wished he could say that he felt bad about the champagne, but he didn't. If anyone was going to toast Bridget, it was going to be him. Quietly, he climbed the stairs. When he got to the top, he heard the water running from the bedroom to his right.

He opened the door, saw the king-size bed and cringed. The bed was one of the reasons he'd picked this house in particular. Romantic, inviting, it reeked of a couple's intimate time together. But not this couple, he thought adamantly.

He made his way to the door that led into the master bathroom and knocked gently. "Bridget," he called, but with water running she obviously didn't hear him. That left him with only one choice.

Richard opened the door and stepped inside. The bathroom was filled with steam from the multiple showerheads, so much so that he could barely see in front of him. He heard her singing to herself and thought that was something he never knew about her. Of course that made sense because they had never shared the same bathroom. Still, he liked the idea of knowing this new intimate detail. More importantly, he liked the idea that he was soon going to know all of her most intimate secrets.

But first they needed to talk.

"Bridget."

He heard her gasp, then he saw her wiping away the steam from the shower door. "Who's there? Brock, so help me God if this is some kind of stunt..."

"Bridget, it's me."

She squinted at him through the glass. "Richard!"

Figuring that if they were going to have the most important conversation of their lives, it was only fair to do it on equal footing. Richard pulled off his cotton shirt, while at the same time kicking off his sneakers.

"Richard, what are you doing here?"

"Stopping you from making a mistake," he said. But that wasn't right. He was here for so much more than that.

His jeans around his ankles now, he stepped out of them and tossed them aside.

"I know you are not thinking about getting into this shower with me."

Since he was thinking exactly that, he asked, "Why not?"

"You're naked! I'm naked. We would be naked together. In a shower."

"I hate to point this out to you when you are obviously in such a frazzled state, but I've seen you like that before."

Richard walked purposefully toward the glass shower door and opened it.

Bridget squeaked and tried to cover herself with a square washcloth, but it was no use. He still got an eyeful of her perfectly shaped body and, for a moment, he was distracted enough to think that maybe their talk could wait. Fifteen, twenty minutes tops, the way he was feeling right now.

"Richard, you can't be here. What if Buzz shows up with the camera and…"

He moved in close to her and placed his fingers over her lips to stop her in midsentence. Then he took a deep breath and tried to control his own hormones for the time being.

"I came here to apologize. I'm really sorry I made you go on the show, Bridge. Will you forgive me?"

Bridget's mind was in a whirl. She had a hard time concentrating on what he was saying. Then again, that might have something to do with the fact that a very naked, very aroused Richard was standing next to her in a shower. "I don't understand."

"I know you hate the spotlight, but I asked you to do it anyway and that was wrong. But I'm here now to find out why you did it."

"Here in this shower?"

"No, here at this house, the shower thing wasn't exactly planned. But at least it's private. Buzz won't dare come in here with the water running. So tell me. The truth. Why did you agree to do the show?"

"The missing girl, and the shot needed to be even, and our deal. Christmas Eve, remember," she replied lamely.

"I remember all of that, but that's not really why you did it. Tell me." He moved even closer to her, their bodies practically touching as the hot water pounded at them from all angles. "Why?"

She knew what he was asking. Which meant he finally must have figured out the truth. And he wanted to hear her admit it. Why? Certainly not so he could tell her that he didn't feel the same way. He wouldn't follow her to this house, sneak inside her shower, make her confess that she was in love with him, only to say tough luck. Would he? She could feel her heart beat excitedly against her ribs as hope blossomed inside her belly.

"You tell me why you came here first."

He scowled at her. "You tell me why you did the show and I'll tell you why I'm here."

She sighed. It was tough trying to play hardball while standing naked in a shower. "I guess I did it because I would pretty much do anything for you," she confessed.

"And why is that?" he pressed.

"I sort of realized that it's probably because I *mmlovemmyou*," she mumbled low enough that the sounded of the water covered her words.

Richard reached behind her and turned off the running water. "What was that last part again?"

"I love you," she said again. She lifted her face up to his, met his eyes and this time said it with all the confidence she had within herself. "I love you, Richard. I probably have for a long time. I just didn't want to admit it to myself. I didn't want anything to change. But then we made love and it did change. And you regretted it."

"I did," he admitted. "At the time. Because I didn't want to admit to myself what I felt for you. What I feel for you," he corrected. "Now ask me what I'm doing here."

"What are you doing here?"

"Here in this shower?"

She laughed and playfully slapped him on his arm. "Richard," she growled menacingly. "Tell me."

"I'm here because I know you love me and not Brock. I'm here because I couldn't stand the idea of you being with him when you should be with me. I'm here because even though it was always right there in front of me, I never saw it. I love you, Bridget."

Tears filled her eyes and she used her hand to brush them away. "What about all that stuff you said about not letting anything interfere with your success? And proving yourself to your family."

"A very wise person pointed out to me that you are my family, Bridge. You support me, you push me, you're proud of me and you love me. That's what family is supposed to be. It's supposed to be about accepting the people in your life for who they are and loving them anyway. So the only thing I want to *prove* anymore is that I love you."

This time she let the tears fall. She felt his arms surround her and the feeling that she was coming home after a long stay away was overwhelming. She hugged him back and the two of them just let themselves be in the moment, just let themselves love and feel loved in return.

That lasted until Richard started kissing her neck. Then Bridget started kissing his mouth. His hands drifted over her body. Her fingers found and caressed the tight firm nipples on his chest. Suddenly, his hands were cupping her bottom and lifting her onto a corner ledge of the shower that put her at exactly the right height to wrap her legs around his waist.

"Should we do this?" she asked as he dipped his head

low and captured her tight pink nipple in his mouth. The feel of him sucking on her breast sent a bolt of hot fire straight down to that aching spot between her legs. The spot she so desperately wanted him to fill again.

Hoping to urge him along, she reached down and caressed the length of his sex and reveled in the way his body shuddered at her slightest touch. She watched him watching her hand move up and down and smiled. He met her smile, but after only a few seconds of her ministrations, he captured her hand and pulled it away from him, first kissing the center of her palm, then placing it on his shoulder.

"Ready?" he asked, his voice throaty and filled with need.

Bridget shivered. "Are you really sure?"

"Oh, yeah. Who's going to catch us?"

Good point, she thought. Brock was probably still out walking and Buzz was with him. They just needed to be quiet. Which was a good idea in theory, but when Richard slid into her wet heat with his thick pulsing erection, she couldn't help but scream out with delight.

"Good?" he asked as he thrust deep.

"Oh, yes! Yes, yes, please don't leave me. Yes. Yes!" She wrapped her arms around his neck and held on for the ride. This was how it was supposed to be, she thought hazily. This was what it meant for two people to be joined physically and emotionally.

She angled her body back and captured his face in her hands. She watched his eyes as he moved deeply inside of her and saw the love and the commitment reflected in his gaze. How had she never seen that before?

"I love you," he whispered against her lips before he tasted her again.

Her body clenched around his shaft and she heard him groan her name as his hips jerked against hers. Just the sound of his love coming from his lips was enough to make her body explode. She tilted her head back against the tile and let the joyous cry she'd been trying to hold back echo off the shower walls.

She felt Richard collapse against her and she struggled to catch her breath even as her body continued to pulse with pleasure.

Pure bliss.

That was until someone began pounding on the door.

"Bridget is that you? Are you okay in there?"

Richard lifted his head and disengaged his body from hers.

"Uh... Yes."

"I heard you screaming," Brock shouted. "And Jenna is here. She's got this crazy idea. I think I need to talk to you about it."

"I'm telling you, I spoke to the limo driver myself. He was paid to another man drive the car up here. You're being duped, Brock. And I won't stand back and let that happen." Jenna's shrill tones could be heard quite clearly through the bathroom door.

Bridget and Richard groaned. "What are we going to do?" she whispered.

"Wait them out?"

"Until tomorrow?"

"You've got a better idea?"

She didn't. The truth was there was nothing to do. Bridget opened the shower door and stepped out with Richard right behind her. She wrapped herself in a towel even as Richard struggled to get his wet legs back in his jeans. He tried jumping to pull them up over his hips, but they wouldn't budge.

"I hear a lot of movement in there," Brock commented. "Are you sure you're okay?"

One last hop and pull and the jeans slid over his hips,

but unfortunately at that moment Richard lost his balance and fell crashing into Bridget. Together they tumbled to the bathroom floor with hands reaching out for anything to grab hold of. The only thing Richard came up with was the tissue dispenser that sat on top of the commode and he sent it crashing to the tile.

"That's it," Brock announced dramatically. "I'm coming in."

"No!" Bridget screamed from underneath Richard, but it was too late.

The door swung open and there on the other side were Brock, Jenna, Buzz and Buzz's camera.

"Oh, yeah," Buzz muttered. "I knew this was going to be good."

"Richard!" Brock shouted. "You? And Bridget?"

"You see, the truth is..." Bridget began then stopped. She was lying naked with only a towel draped about her body, with Richard on top of her dressed only in a pair of damp jeans. There really was no explaining this. Richard rolled off her and got to his feet. Then he stepped in front of her so she could get up and adjust her towel without giving the world a peek at her goodies.

"The truth is you are a slut," Jenna fired at her.

"Do I need to get tough with you again?" Bridget challenged.

"See," Jenna screeched, even as she managed to flip her hair in a perfect arc over her shoulder. "I told you she was unstable, Brock. That's why I had to come. To protect you, don't you see?"

Brock left the bathroom and sat heavily on the bed. He put his face in his hands and after a few seconds, when he lifted his head again, there were actual tears in his eyes.

Wow, Bridget thought. He was better than she gave him credit for.

"I thought I loved you," he began. "I thought you loved me. But all this time it was him. That's why he was at the restaurant. And all of that talk about falling for me. That was just to make him jealous. Wasn't it? Wasn't it?"

Going along with the scene, Bridget hung her head shamefully and nodded.

Jenna ran over and sat next to Brock, reaching for his hand. "It's okay though. You learned the truth in time. Now it's just the two of us. And I would never cheat on you. Ever."

Brock shook his head. "I can't think about that now. Can't you see I'm in pain? I've been betrayed."

He got up and left the room and Jenna followed. "Wait, Brock," she called after him. "I can heal you. I know I can."

Buzz chuckled and turned off the camera. "Now that's drama."

"You knew it was me in the car?" Richard asked, confirming what he'd already suspected.

"Yep. Just be grateful I didn't catch you two in a more *compromising* situation. The audience is going to love this. Now I need to go film a grieving Brock. See you both back in the city."

"I can't believe this," Bridget moaned once it was just the two of them again. "My family is going to see that."

"See what? You look cute in a towel." Richard wrapped his arms around her to nuzzle her neck. "Hey, you don't think Brock was really upset about us, do you?"

"I think Brock deserves a daytime Emmy for his performance." She turned around in his arms and circled his waist with her hands. "So what happens now?"

"We go home."

Home. For the first time, for both of them, it had a really nice ring to it.

"Sounds good."

"Or since Buzz is going to be off filming Brock for a while...we could make use of this bed."

Bridget looked at the bed, then looked back at Richard. She shimmied a little and the towel came loose and dropped to her feet. "Sounds better."

EPILOGUE

TOGETHER, Bridget and Richard snuggled in Richard's bed as they once again watched the videotape of what had turned out to be the final episode of *Who Wants to Marry a Heartthrob?*

The scene unfolded before them with a clarity they only had been able to speculate about when they had been part of the show.

"Jenna? What are you doing here?" Brock asked, opening the front door of the cabin.

Jenna, wearing a striking peach ensemble, sans neck brace, flipped her hair back and played the part of a distraught friend trying to win the heart of the hero. "I had to tell you that I think...I think...Bridget is cheating on you."

"Don't be ridiculous. She said she loved me. Is this some ploy to get me to pick you?"

"No, I swear," Jenna pleaded with him. "At first, I just was worried about you being alone with her so I called the limo company to find out where you were staying and they told me that someone had paid the driver to let him take the car instead. I knew then that I had to come and warn you."

"This is good stuff," Bridget noted as she watched the TV. "I think I need to start watching soap operas more often."

"Shh," Richard hushed her. "My favorite part is coming up."

"Oh, yes. Yes, yes!"

The sound of Bridget screaming in ecstasy not only echoed off the shower walls, but also apparently filtered down the stairs throughout the whole house. Mortified, she pulled the covers over her head.

"What was that?" Brock asked, evidently confused. Another unmistakable scream filled the house. "I think Bridget might be in trouble."

"Not exactly," Richard noted as the show continued to play out.

Brock and Jenna ran up the stairs and Bridget didn't need to watch what happened next. She remembered vividly appearing in front of them, and now all of America, in nothing more than a towel.

"Do we have to watch this?" she wanted to know, peeking her head out from underneath the covers just in time to see her flushed faced fill the screen, while a shirtless Richard, who was draped on top of her, looked to all the world like a man who had just gotten laid.

Which, of course, he had.

Richard chuckled. "Come on, this is good. And look where it got us. Dan and Don watched this tape and said anyone willing to go to such lengths for an ad campaign was the man they wanted to do business with from here on out."

"What about the lengths I went to? You can see the tops of my breasts in that towel."

"Of course they meant both of us," he said, as his eyes focused on the television.

"Richard, why are you staring at the TV? You can see my breasts anytime you want."

"Yeah, but they look bigger on TV."

She elbowed him in the stomach and he let out a satisfactory woof.

"I'm kidding," he chuckled. "But tell me, have you decided about the job yet?"

After much consideration and a lot of talking between them, Richard had decided that having his own agency was something he wanted for himself, and not just as a way to prove himself to his family. Having his own agency not only would give him the creative freedom he desired, but it also would give him a chance to spend time getting his cartoon published. With Bridget squarely in his corner rooting him on, he didn't think he could fail.

The question that remained was now that they were lovers, should she still work for him?

"I'm still not sure. Yes, I want to be your vice president. But I don't think it would be the best idea for us to work together."

"Why not?"

"Because technically you would still be my boss and as my boss you would get to tell me what to do."

"Yes, but as my girlfriend you get to tell me what to do," Richard pointed out.

"True."

"Hold that thought. Okay, this is it," Richard said pointing to the screen.

The cabin was gone, replaced by a shot of Brock and the host, Chuck, once again sitting in the all-white living room in the house on Long Island.

"So tell us Brock, in your own words, why did you decide to leave the show so close to the end?"

"I just couldn't deal with Bridget's betrayal. It really rocked me. Deeply. You know what I'm saying. On a deep level."

"He's so full of it," she muttered. "He needed to get back on the set of *The Many Days of Life*."

"Shh."

"How is a guy supposed to recover from that?" Brock continued. "I can't see myself ever deciding to marry anyone. Ever."

"At least not a woman," Bridget murmured.

"What was that?"

Since the show was over, she didn't imagine there would be any harm in telling him now. "Richard, what if I told you that Brock is actually gay?"

He burst out laughing. "Yeah, right. America's Daytime Heartthrob is gay. Will you get serious? You and Raquel are both so wrong about that."

"Are we?"

"I think I would know if he was gay," Richard assured her.

"Of course you would. What was I thinking?"

"Such a shame," Chuck commented sympathetically as he patted Brock on the shoulder. "What will you do now?"

"Funny you should mention that, Chuck. I'll be returning to my role as Chief Surgeon, Dr. Noah Vanderhorn on *The Many Days of Life*. I plan on pouring myself into my work."

"You are aware, of course, that Jenna has also been cast to play a part on that show. Will it be comfortable for you working with her?"

"Jenna and I are professionals. I don't see us having a problem."

"And have you even spoken to Bridget since that awful day at the cabin?"

Brock feigned choking back some tears. "I can't. Maybe someday I can ask her why? Why she betrayed me the way she did. Just not now."

"What a load of horse manure," Bridget shouted. "I'm telling you, we had it all set up. He knew I was in love with you. This is all just an act."

"Yeah, but it's great for ratings."

The show ended and Richard turned off the TV. He sank

back down into the bed and pulled Bridget into his arms. "It looks like it worked out for everyone in the end. So let's settle this last thing once and for all. If you don't work for me, we won't get to have our Wednesday deli lunches."

"True," she muttered.

"If you don't work for me, we won't get to have our Monday nooners on the desk."

She smiled. "We never had Monday nooners on the desk."

"I was thinking of starting a new tradition."

"I see."

Richard sighed. "All right. What is it going to take?"

And those had been the magic words she'd been waiting for. "It seems that my parents have this crazy idea that people who live together should actually be married."

"I thought we agreed that we weren't going to cater to our parents' expectations anymore."

"And we're not. Except for this one thing," Bridget finished weakly. "Besides it's only fair."

"How do you figure?"

"Well, everyone got something out of this. Dan and Don had a successful show. You're getting your own agency. Even Brock and Jenna got what they wanted. But what about me? I didn't get my heartthrob."

"You got me!"

"Yes, but I didn't get a wedding." She waited a beat and then asked. "If you want me to be your partner, then I think I should be your partner...in every sense of the word. Don't you?"

Richard closed his eyes and moaned. "I should have guessed you were going to play tough."

"It's a little game I like to play called hardball..."

"I know. I know. And I'm the one who taught you. Fine. We get married. You become my business partner...and I get my Monday nooners."

"Deal."

"Deal."

There was a pause then as Bridget considered what had just happened. Basically she'd guilted and blackmailed Richard into marrying her. In all honesty, that wasn't exactly fair, either. What if he wasn't ready to get married? What if he wanted to live together for a while to see where this relationship was going first?

"Oh, and Bridge?"

"Yes?" she asked, afraid that he was about to call her on what she'd done. If he did, she would have to let him off the hook. She did have some ethics after all.

He rolled over on his side and opened the drawer on the night table. When he rolled back, he had a ring box in his hand. "I guess if we're going to be married, you should wear the engagement ring I got you."

He opened the box and slid the beautiful solitaire diamond on her finger. Instantly, she felt the tears back up in her throat. "That was probably the most romantic proposal ever," she sniffed.

"What can I say? I'm discovering new depths to me every day. Now, there you see, you do get to marry a heartthrob after all."

She considered pointing out that he wasn't exactly *heartthrob* material. But then again, he did make her heart throb. And that was all that mattered.

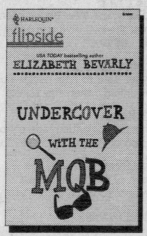

e‖HARLEQUIN.com

The Ultimate Destination for Women's Fiction

For **FREE online reading,** visit
www.eHarlequin.com now and enjoy:

Online Reads
Read **Daily** and **Weekly** chapters from
our Internet-exclusive stories by your
favorite authors.

Interactive Novels
Cast your vote to help decide how these
stories unfold…then stay tuned!

Quick Reads
For shorter romantic reads, try our
collection of Poems, Toasts, & More!

Online Read Library
Miss one of our online reads?
Come here to catch up!

Reading Groups
Discuss, share and rave with other
community members!

For great reading online,
visit www.eHarlequin.com today!